Secrets of a Schoolyard Millionaire

Nat Amoore

ROCK THE BOAT

A Rock the Boat Book

First published in Great Britain and America by Rock the Boat,
an imprint of Oneworld Publications, 2021

Text © Nat Amoore, 2019, 2021
Illustration © Diane Ewen, 2021
First published by Penguin Random House Australia Pty Ltd

The moral right of Nat Amoore and Diane Ewen to be identified as
the author and illustrator of this work respectively has been asserted by
them in accordance with the Copyright, Designs and Patents Act 1988

ISBN 978-0-86154-039-6 (paperback)
ISBN 978-0-86154-040-2 (ebook)

Printed and bound in Great Britain by Clays Ltd, Elcograf S.p.A.

Oneworld Publications
10 Bloomsbury Street
London WC1B 3SR
England

Stay up to date with the latest books,
special offers, and exclusive content from
Rock the Boat with our newsletter

Sign up on our website
oneworld-publications.com/rtb

Praise for *Secrets*

"Any fan of the Treehouse the storeys, contraptions and rooms that would be present in their own treehouses, and Nat Amoore's debut novel posits an equally enticing prospect: what would you do if you found a million dollars in your backyard?"

Guardian

"Top tier fun. Fast-paced, clever and completely hilarious with the BEST cast of characters, including two incredible young entrepreneurs. Packed with life lessons too. LOVE IT TO BITS."

Rashmi Sirdeshpande, author of *Dosh*

"A thoroughly entertaining read that children will storm through. Wise advice, lots of laughs and an important message about the things money can't buy... Laughs, family, friendships and a thrilling adventure – *Secrets of a Schoolyard Millionaire* has it all."

Jen Carney, author of *The Accidental Diary of B.U.G.*

"Pure brilliance and fun, *Secrets of a Schoolyard Millionaire* is a triumphant debut by Nat Amoore, worth its weight in bank notes."

Dimity Powell, author of *The Fix-It Man*

"*Secrets of a Schoolyard Millionaire* is a lively, precocious book for readers with big ideas and big hearts."

Readings

"*Secrets of a Schoolyard Millionaire* is pure fun and will appeal to both reluctant and keen readers alike... Amoore's take is contemporary, super quirky and a rollicking adventure."

Children's Books Daily

"This book had me from the first page, pulling me into Tess's world... This is a fresh, exciting and thrilling read for kids."

Kids' Book Review

For Cathie – because with friends like you,
who needs smiley faces?

1

The End

Sometimes you learn a lesson . . . and sometimes you have to teach yourself one.

The first Monday in April happened a bit like this. It might sound like a scene from a movie, but that's because it *was* like a scene from a movie.

I'm walking down the school corridor – I'm pretty sure in slow motion – with a look of determination on my face. I always look determined. The other kids stand in front of the lockers, gawking at me as I pass. I ignore them, staring straight ahead. There's theme music playing in my head – "Money" by Pink Floyd. Don't know it? Google it. Great song. Mum and Dad only listen to Gold 104 at home. They say music was so much better before I was born. I totally agree.

So anyway, I'm walking down the corridor – in slow motion – and on one side of me is my teacher, Mr Deery, and on the other, the headteacher, Mrs Keiren. They don't look happy – although Mrs Keiren never looks happy.

More kids turn to stare. Their mouths drop open. They look like rows of blue and white uniformed goldfish. What's so stare-worthy about a Year Five walking down the hall with her teacher and the head? Not much, actually. So it's probably the other people behind us who are getting all the attention.

My teachers are flanked by two uniformed police officers. They don't look very happy either.

And it's me everyone is unhappy with.

I catch Toby's eye as I pass him. He looks terrified. He has a Chihuahua quality about him – head too big for his body, eyes too big for his head – but when he's scared he shakes like one too. I try to give him a look that says "everything will be ok", but I think he wants to crawl into his locker with his books. He'd probably fit.

I stop in front of my locker. The school corridor is almost silent – I'm pretty sure I can still hear Toby shaking.

"Is this your locker, Miss Heckleston?" says the big police officer.

"That's what it says," I say, pointing to the gold-plated, engraved nametag I bought for myself. It's the kind that executives have on their office desk. I thought it would give a more professional look than the paper ones that just slide into the slot. All the other kids handwrite their names on those and put stickers all over them. But not me. Rachel Zoe (Don't know her? Google her!) once said, "Style is a way of saying who you are without having to speak". My locker says a lot.

"That's enough, Tess," says Mrs Keiren. "Just answer the officer."

I do everything I can to stop my eyes from rolling. Mum says I roll my eyes way too much.

"Yes, officer, sir," I say. "This is my locker."

"Open it," says the bigger officer. Apparently police only come in two sizes – big and bigger.

I turn to Mr Deery. He stares back at me with a look of disappointment and sympathy. I'm not a fan of that look. He nods towards the locker.

I sigh and slowly turn to face it. I've read up on my rights when it comes to school searches and confiscations on lawstuff.org.au (you should *always* know your rights), so I know that my locker is school property and I can't argue with this demand. Anyway, I got myself into this and the time has come for me to fess up.

I reach up and select the combination on my padlock.

The kids watching are too scared to come any closer, but I can feel them craning their necks like nosy emus, trying to get a glimpse. The two teachers and two police officers move in closer.

I slide the padlock out of the iron loop and pause. See, I know what happens next. And I know It's been coming. But I feel like I need just one more minute before it all changes.

"Open it!" say the officers behind me.

I take a breath and swing the steel door open.

I hear the entire school gasp behind me as out tumbles . . . one million dollars.

I'm the kind of kid who likes to get straight to the point. That's how this story ends.

There are no surprises.

I totally get busted.

Don't hang around hoping that I'm going to ride off into the sunset with my bag-loads of cash. It doesn't happen. That kind of stuff doesn't happen in the real world. Life doesn't always tie up neatly in a bow. But the last few months have been a real . . . experience. And experience is pretty much the only thing you can't Google.

I have a crazy story. I made loads of mistakes, but I learnt a lot. So stick with me, and you might as well.

2

The Beginning
Part one

These things usually start with "I was just your normal, average ten-year-old" – well, not this time. I am, and have always been, anything but normal and/or average. I can't think of anything worse than being average. Be weird, be strange, be extraordinary, be exceptional – NEVER be average.

My name is Tess Heckleston. I'm in Year Five at Watterson Primary. My best friend is Toby Baker (he's also anything but average – he's one of the weirdest people I know). I live with Mum, Dad and four brothers and sisters, and I'm smack bang in the middle.

There! Boring stuff done.

Now here's what you really want to know. How does a ten-year-old end up with bucketloads of cash in her school locker?

I'm what people would call an entrepreneur. Know what that means? No? Google it. In fact, here's my first tip.

TIP 1

USE GOOGLE!

You'll hear adults talk all the time about how our generation "spends too much time on their screens". Adults don't always know what they're talking about. If you're on the computer playing games or watching cat videos, then yeah, you're frying your brain. But Google is the greatest thing ever. You can literally Google how to do anything. If you don't know something, Google it. It will make you smarter.

So I'm an entrepreneur. I come up with ideas. And most of my ideas are about how to make money. Money is important in life. You need it to do almost everything. Even eat. Unless you own a farm and grow your own food. Actually no, even that costs money.

In Year Three, I ran a sports gambling ring down on the back field. Kids could bet their lunch or pocket money on different sporting events, which I organised. You could bet on almost anything – running races, wrestling matches, tree climbing. I learnt about odds and how betting works, and Toby did the maths. He's the numbers guy in this team. I think we made about a hundred dollars before Ms Jensen shut us down because Sam McVean cried to her about losing his lunch money on a monkey bar challenge. Then we had to give all the money back *and* apologise to the kids and their parents *and* be on playground duty for two weeks. So when you hear things like "everyone loses in gambling", it's true. We spent a lot of time and energy to end up with nothing . . . I think that pretty much sums up gambling for me. So we decided no more gambling scams, and we moved onto proper businesses from there.

In Year Four, I ran a spy agency out of the swimming pool changing room during winter. I had a staff of five spies who could be hired to follow someone around for a whole lunchtime and report back on their movements. Toby wrote out and delivered the reports, and the profit margin was good until the swimming pool opened in summer and we had to move out of our office. Rent overheads are always a huge business concern.

Earlier this year we started Homework Handled. Toby was worried this business was sort of "cheating". I can't say he was wrong, but I liked to think of it more as a service. For a small fee – including a commission, of course – I paired kids who needed their homework done with kids who liked doing homework. See, some kids have busy social lives and not enough time to do their homework. And some kids love homework and can't get enough. I simply put supply and demand together – it's just smart business.

I explained to Toby that technically we weren't doing anything wrong. *We* weren't getting our homework done for us AND *we* weren't doing other kids' homework.

Toby said it was "shady".

I said it was "creative".

Toby didn't agree and closed that business down pretty quick.

But that's the thing with money. Sometimes you have to be creative. My mum works a regular job and Dad takes care of us kids. We have an OK house, but at the end of every month they're always scraping money together to try and pay all the bills and stuff. That's because working like a normal person is *not* creative. When I'm older there will be no scraping. I'm going to buy Mum and Dad a house and take care of all their bills so they don't have to worry about that stuff. It'll be a big house, so all my brothers and sisters can live there too. I'll have my own house, of course, but no one will be worrying about money. No one.

Not even Toby. Not that Toby really worries about money, which is weird, because Toby worries about almost everything. He's a nervous kind of kid. But he's *so* smart. Probably smarter than me. Just quieter. People think I don't appreciate Toby, but they're wrong. I know, without a doubt, that Toby is the best friend a person could have. I just don't tell him that, because that kind of stuff is all a bit warm and fuzzy for me.

I want to show my appreciation for Toby here, though, so I think I'll give him his own bit. It's the least he deserves after what he did for me.

3

Toby

TIP 2

GET A BEST FRIEND LIKE TOBY!
Toby is very, very useful. He's great at writing
lists, organising things, taking notes, making
sure our calendar is up to date, keeping our
accounts in order and listening to all my great
ideas. He's also been my best friend since we
were three, so there's history.

Friendship is about trust. And I totally trust Toby.
I tell him all my ingenious business schemes,

and I never worry that he'll steal them and make millions without me. He lives three houses down and across the road from me. It's hard to explain a seven-year friendship in just a few words. It's like a lifetime of stuff!

Toby turned ten at the end of last year. I think how he spent his birthday explains my friend pretty well.

It was a Wednesday, so Toby had his advanced classes – yeah, OK, he's better at school than me, BUT if they would just add advanced business studies to the timetable like I asked, I'd show him a thing or two. Anyway, I finally found him at break. In the library! I should have guessed. Toby would spend his whole day there if he could. He was staring at a computer screen and didn't even see me come in. I snuck up behind him and dropped a plastic container down in front of him.

"Happy Birthday!"

He spun round. "Is that what I think it is?"

"Sure is. Dad said he put extra jalapeños this time. You didn't bring lunch, right?"

"Of course not. My mums know better than that."

It's a tradition that's been going forever. Dad makes Toby's lunch for him on his birthday. Always. Even when he's at school. Toby's mums are super cool but they aren't great cooks. The last two years Dad's made Toby enchiladas.

Toby opened the lid and breathed his lunch in. "So good."

Coming from a family of five, we don't get birthday parties. That would be crazy expensive for Mum and Dad. But we do get to choose everything on our birthday. What we want for lunch. What we watch on TV. What we do that day (except if it's school – school is non-negotiable). Toby's family has taken on our tradition, even though they only have one kid.

"OK, so what was for breakfast?" I asked.

"Banana pancakes."

"Nice! And presents before or after school?"

"Before."

"So? What did you get?"

Toby grinned at me and pointed to the computer screen.

A small girl who I guessed was about seven smiled back at me. Above her, it said:

ANYA IS A GIRL FROM KENYA WHO NEEDS $253 TO FUND A HERNIA OPERATION.

"Watsi, Toby? Really? For your birthday?"

Toby nodded. "I get to pick anybody. I think I'm going to go with Anya."

Toby discovered watsi.org a couple of months before his birthday. Check it out, it's pretty cool. They have all these people from other countries who need operations. It shows how much each one is going to cost, and you can donate money to make it happen. Toby always uses his pocket money and his share of our profits on that website. He gives his cash to his mums and they use their credit card to donate online. I wish I had a credit card. He used the money we made at last year's garage sale to get some kid in Cambodia an eye operation. I used it to buy Scott Pape's book *The Barefoot Investor*. Yeah – Toby's a better person than me.

I dragged Toby out of the library and down to the lower playground. Dad had made some cupcakes, so I'd set up a little party table for Toby and a few of our friends were waiting. We sang "Happy Birthday" and munched on Dad's cupcakes.

In the next class, we did maths with Mr Deery. Which pretty much meant Toby was as happy as he could be. Toby is REALLY good at numbers. Like Ada Lovelace good. If you don't know Ada Lovelace – Google her! She was pretty much the world's first computer programmer and is seriously awesome. So Toby is *that* good. He takes care of all our accounts for our businesses and makes sure we're always running at a profit. He keeps track of everything – every cent we spend or earn, every receipt – and he *never* makes a mistake.

Anyway, part of me thinks maybe Mr Deery added in some extra maths just because it was Toby's birthday. Worst of all, it was fractions.

"Does anyone know how we subtract unlike fractions?" asked Mr Deery.

I knew Toby knew, but he never puts his hand up in class.

"How about the birthday boy?" It seemed Mr Deery also knew that Toby knew.

Before Toby even got a chance to answer, the whole class broke out into a second round of "Happy Birthday".

Next was swimming class. Wednesday is a good day for Toby's birthday. He loves swimming.

"Can I touch it?" said Sarah Krykov.

Toby shrugged. "Sure." This was pretty typical at swim class. Toby has this cool scar that runs straight down the middle of his chest. The other kids go crazy for it.

"I wish I could have a tan like yours, Toby," said Sarah as she poked at his chest. "My mum covers me in so much sunscreen, I'm not sure my skin has ever even really seen the sun."

I can see why, though. Sarah is as pale as can be. Standing next to Toby doesn't help her either.

Toby was born in Bolivia. He says he's "Bolivian/ Australian". I suggested "Bolstralian", but he didn't think it would catch on. I like having a Bolivian/ Australian best friend. It makes me feel worldly. And seeing as I've never been to another country and technically Toby has, I reckon he's more cultured than me. He says that's ridiculous because his mums adopted him and brought him to Australia when he was six months old, so he doesn't remember anything. I was hoping maybe subconsciously he might remember how to speak Bolivian, but no luck there either. Plus I Googled it and they speak Spanish in Bolivia, and I know from our *Dora the Explorer* phase that Toby definitely doesn't speak Spanish.

So the story goes something like . . . Toby was in an orphanage in Bolivia and needed some life-saving operation on his heart. His mums were doing work for a charity here in Australia that funded these operations. Then they took a trip to Bolivia to visit some of the people they had helped, saw Toby's squishy little face, fell in love with him and brought him home. I'm sure there's more to it than that, but it's handy to summarise. So not only is Toby worldly, but he has that super-cool scar on his chest from his operation. I wish I had a cool scar. One of my fingers is a little bent, but that's about it.

After swimming was lunch, where Toby oohed and aahed over Dad's enchiladas. More classes then, FINALLY, home time.

Now, I have to make this very clear. On his birthday Toby could do anything, right? Choose anything. Go anywhere. Eat anything. Watch anything. And this includes his mums, my parents and all my siblings because we're pretty much just one big family.

You know what Toby chose to do that night?

We all volunteered at Cook4Good, making food for people with no homes or money.

Yup – that's Toby.

4

The Beginning
Part Two

So me and Toby are a team. Our number one aim is to get rich, and get rich soon. OK, that's my aim, but Toby is totally on board.

We always talk about all the great things we could do if we had loads of money. I'd definitely put a waterslide in our school pool and make sure all the kids have at least one treat in their lunch boxes. A REAL treat – not like my lunch box where Dad puts in an apple with a sticky note that says "Imagine it's a Mars Bar".

Toby has some ideas too. You know, helping others and stuff like that.

We keep most of our ideas to ourselves because adults don't really get it. I mean, we're not talking about loose change. We want to make thousands. Hundreds of thousands!

Adults just think too small.

A while back at school, the bell rang for lunch. Toby and I had to rush out. We were running a mini-tuckshop that week. We had pooled our pocket money and used Toby's mums' Costco card to buy snacks in bulk. We were selling them from the bike shed way cheaper than the kids could buy them at the school tuckshop, but still at a profit for us, so it was win-win. Every day, even when we rushed to the shed, there was already a line of kids waiting.

But this day, Mr Deery stopped me on the way out.

"Hey, Tess, I saw something that I thought you might be interested in." He handed me a flyer. Plastered across the top in bright yellow block letters was *Kids Business*. "It's a competition for primary school kids to come up with a business idea. I know you're really into that sort of thing. Always reading those 'how to be a success' books. I thought you could enter."

I tried my best not to roll my eyes. Mr Deery is nice, but he has no clue.

"Maybe you could do a cake stall. Or do some chores for people in the neighbourhood."

Don't roll, eyes. Don't roll!

"And there's prize money for the best business idea. Look!" Mr Deery poked his finger at the flyer. "Ten dollars!"

I looked at his beaming face. Seriously. No idea. "Awesome, Mr Deery, thanks! Sounds great."

I turned to Toby, who was nodding along like one of those bobble heads on a car dashboard. *Too much fake enthusiasm, Toby!*

"I thought it would be right up your street, Tess." Mr Deery looked awfully proud of himself. "You're such a little go-getter. You'll be running this country one day."

I smiled my biggest smile back at him. "You bet, Mr Deery. Thanks! Gotta go."

"Absolutely, Tess. And if you need any help coming up with ideas, just let me know. See if we can't win you that ten dollars."

"Uh huh." I grabbed Toby and dragged him off. When we were at a safe distance, I let my eyes roll.

It was such a relief. "Ten dollars," I scoffed. I screwed up the flyer and handed it to Toby, who dropped it in the recycling bin.

That lunch we made a total profit of eighty-three dollars in forty-five minutes at our mini-tuckshop.

TIP 3

ADULTS CAN UNDERESTIMATE KIDS.
It's not their fault. They're only adults, they have a lot to learn. Be patient and understand they're just doing their best.

And so I thought I had it sorted. Business ideas and get-rich-quick schemes. I read all the books, watched all the movies and I was super sure that it was just a matter of trying different things until I finally hit it big time.

Then in February, something happened that changed everything.

5

February

I can hear the mayhem behind the front door before I even turn the handle. Welcome to the Heckleston Hothouse – that's what Dad calls it.

I swing the door open to reveal my family. The Heckle-tribe.

Jake is chewing on the edge of the sofa. Jake is always chewing on some piece of furniture.

So right now you're probably thinking Jake is our dog, right? Nope. Jake is my youngest brother. He's one and a half and is teething. Dad's tried a whole heap of teething toys but Jake still prefers the furniture. He's a weird kid.

Olivia is sitting cross-legged on the lounge room floor with her head buried in a book that weighs more than she does. To say she's a bookworm is a serious understatement. She's really clever. She's only seven, but if it wasn't for Google, she'd already be smarter than me.

Dane is teaching Butthead to play dead. Dane's my older brother. He's twelve, although sometimes I find that very hard to believe. Butthead is his dog. Dane got Butthead from the animal shelter for his birthday, so he's Dane's dog, which means none of us had *any* say in his name. I just want to make that very clear. Dane's a doofus and so is Butthead. They're perfect for each other.

And last of all, there's Sash. She has her ears plugged with headphones and is frantically flicking away at her iPhone. This is a good thing, because Sash only has two modes. Plugged and unplugged. This is plugged. She's quiet, calm and still. Then there's unplugged, where she screams and rants and cries and fights with Mum and storms from room to room slamming doors. We must all be grateful when Sash is plugged.

Dad's in the kitchen. He's already started getting dinner ready. Mum won't be home until eight at the earliest. Mostly she comes home after we've already eaten. The radio is blaring as Dad dances around the kitchen to "Handle With Care" by The Traveling Wilburys. The song is great. Dad's dancing is not.

I walk inside, ignored by everyone except Dad.

"Hey, Tess! How was school?" he calls from the kitchen.

"Good thanks, Dad," I call back without stopping.

"Fettuccine boscaiola for dinner."

"Sounds great." I go upstairs and close my bedroom door behind me, shutting out the Heckle-tribe.

TIP 4

_____

DON'T BE A MIDDLE CHILD!

OK, so you may not have a lot of control over this, but try to avoid it if you can. It's a tough gig. If you do find yourself in this position, make the most of it. When all seems doomed, just remember . . . Bill Gates was a middle child. If you don't know who Bill Gates is, see **Tip 1**.

_____

My mum and dad don't have a lot of time – and they have a lot of kids. As far as the kids in the family go, I definitely take the least effort. While Mum and Dad deal with my siblings, I get left to my own devices. And I like it like that. I love my family, but they're hard work. And they're always around. I mean, literally, there are so many of them you can't escape.

But at least I have my own room.

My room is the only room upstairs and at the back of the house. It's smaller than the others, but it's quieter so it suits me fine. It's got a huge window that looks down over our back garden, and also down into Scotty's back garden.

Scotty is our neighbour. Mum does *not* like Scotty. She says she wishes we had more money so we could afford to move to a "better neighbourhood" and "away from the riffraff". But I think Scotty is interesting. Strange, but interesting.

Our garden is pretty big and I'm the only one who really uses it. Jake doesn't play out there much because there's no furniture to chew on. Olivia's an inside kid – it's hard to read in the sun, she says. Dane takes Butthead to the park and Sash only goes from school to the sofa to her room and back again. So that leaves the garden all for me.

There, I have my trampoline and my treasure chest.

My treasure chest is where I keep all my important stuff. When you have four siblings, you can't keep important stuff in your room. In fact . . .

TIP 5

KEEP YOUR IMPORTANT STUFF SOMEWHERE SAFE!

Everyone's important stuff is different. You decide what your important stuff is, then keep it somewhere safe. If you don't take care of your important stuff and then it goes missing, it's your own fault. As you may have worked out from my story so far, your school locker is NOT the place for your important stuff.

My treasure chest is just a big toy pirate's chest. It's bedazzled with fake gold and jewels and pushed up against the fence, just next to my trampoline. I've had it since I was little. I think it used to be Dane's. When you lift up the lid it looks like it's full of balls and Frisbees and other outdoor toys, BUT . . . my treasure chest has a false bottom. Underneath the junk, if you lift up the base, there's another space hidden below. That's where I keep the cool stuff. What was there before my story isn't important. But my treasure chest is.

My trampoline I use for bouncing – no surprises there, right? I find bouncing therapeutic. Therapeutic? Google it. You should find something that's therapeutic for you. It will help you through life. I go to bounce when I need to think, and a little bit when I want to see what's going on at Scotty's.

6

Scotty

Scotty is kind of skinny. Mum calls him "scrawny". He has a lot of tattoos. And I mean, a lot. They come right down to his hands like shirtsleeves and creep out of his collar and up his neck and curl around his ears. It looks like they're taking over his body. They're all so squashed together that I can't really tell what they are, exactly, but one is definitely a dragon. Its head pokes out from Scotty's shirt and its jaws open wide under his chin. It looks like it's trying to swallow Scotty's head.

Mum said never, under any circumstances, was I ever allowed to talk to Scotty.

But I have talked to Scotty. A few times. I just never told Mum.

The first time I spoke to Scotty, I was on my trampoline. I could only see over the fence when I bounced.

UP

Scotty was in the back garden with a group of his friends.

DOWN

UP

They almost all had tattoos and they were having a barbeque.

DOWN

UP

There was a bundle of money on the table.

DOWN

UP

It must have been about $1000.

DOWN

UP

Maybe more.

DOWN

UP

Scotty was staring straight at me.

I stopped bouncing. I stayed crouched down on the black canvas of the trampoline, the rough material prickling my hands.

After what seemed like forever, I slowly stood up. I was too scared to bounce again. What if he was right there? But I really wanted to get another look at that money.

Just then a tattooed hand reached up and over the fence. It dropped a can of soft drink into my garden.

I stared at it.

"Um, thanks," I said softly.

There was no response.

A few seconds passed and then the hand reached over again – this time dropping a twenty-dollar note.

"Whoa! Awesome. Thanks." I grabbed the twenty.

Scotty laughed from the other side of the fence. "Keep the change," he said, and I heard him walk off.

The party went late into the night. Both the can of soft drink and the twenty went into my treasure chest.

$

That was my first contact with Scotty . . . but not my last.

Spoiler alert. Scotty does not turn out to be a misunderstood but lovable character from over the fence. Scotty is a *bad guy*. When Mum said I shouldn't talk to him, she was right. I should have listened to my mum.

TIP 6

DON'T TALK TO STRANGERS AND DON'T TAKE STUFF FROM THEM!
Your parents are right with this one. Sometimes strangers can be good, but sometimes they can be bad. Unfortunately, you can't know which is which.

After the drink and twenty incident, I spoke to Scotty a few more times. We didn't have long conversations. We weren't friends or anything. Just a few words here and there. He gave me more stuff and I hid it away. I knew that he had seen my treasure chest, but I felt like he wouldn't tell anyone. I mean, I didn't tell anyone his secrets. And I saw a lot.

One time, I was bouncing. And watching. People were coming to see Scotty. Lots of different people. They were giving him money. Lots and lots of money. So much that it made me wonder if it was even real.

I guess he was running a business, but I wasn't sure what. He didn't seem to be doing anything for the money. It looked like a great business model. One man gave Scotty some money, but Scotty didn't seem to think it was enough. He grabbed the man.

UP
Scotty gripped the man's shirt under his chin.
DOWN

UP

Scotty was shouting something at the man.

DOWN

UP

The man was pleading with Scotty.

DOWN

UP

Scotty was saying something to his friends.

DOWN

UP

The man was gone.

Scotty looked over at me bouncing. He walked towards me. I stopped bouncing and got off the trampoline. My treasure chest was next to the fence, so I climbed on top of it and looked over. There was Scotty. He raised his finger to his lips, passed me a twenty-dollar note and said, "Shhhh."

I took the money and nodded.

Looking back now, of course I can see it was stupid.

But back then I had a way of convincing myself something wasn't that bad even when I knew it was wrong. Like Homework Handled. I knew that was wrong too. But I told myself it was OK because I wanted to believe it was. That's a really dumb thing to do. So here's a big one . . .

TIP 7

IF SOMETHING FEELS WRONG, IT IS WRONG!

You have to listen to that little voice that tells you when you're doing the wrong thing. It's called your conscience, and it's there for a reason. It's that little voice that makes you a good person, and, above everything else, you must be a good person.

But yeah, I ignored the voice. And I ignored my mum. Because I thought I knew better, and I thought I could handle it. People are always saying I'm "so independent" and "so beyond my years". I believed that. I believed I knew best.

I was wrong.

7

Back to February

So Dad is downstairs cooking fettuccine boscaiola and my brothers and sisters are doing what they do. I'm upstairs in my room, looking out of my window and down into Scotty's garden.

There are a lot of people at his house. There are always people coming and going, but this time I think he must be having another party.

"DINNER IS SERVED, HECKLE-TRIBE!" Dad calls from downstairs.

I head down. Mum's bag isn't on her hook, so I know she's not home yet. She usually comes home during dinner on a good day. After dinner on a bad day. After bedtime on a really bad day.

I prise Jake's teeth off the coffee table and put him in his high chair, strapping him in tight like I'm sending him to the moon. He wriggles like one of those wavy blow-up men at a car dealer. I give him a book to chew on and start setting the table.

"Thanks, Tessels," says Dad. I give him my "don't call me that" look. Cute nicknames do NOT demand respect in the business world.

TIP 8

DON'T HAVE A CUTESY NICKNAME. ESPECIALLY ONE THAT MAKES YOUR NAME LONGER. THAT'S JUST RIDICULOUS.

Have you EVER heard of a successful business person with a cutesy nickname? Does Mark Zuckerberg go by Marky? Is Ronesha Byng all like, "Oh, just call me Ro-Ro?" The answer is no.

Dad ignores the look. He always does.

"Got any homework tonight?" he asks.

"Done it already."

"Didn't need any help?" He smiles at me as he drains the fettuccine.

You might not get it, but this is Dad making a joke. My dad is great. He's funny, tells awesome bedtime stories and makes the best pasta in the world, but he hasn't helped me with my homework since I was in Year One. Actually, I kind of help him with his.

"I fixed your email, Dad," I say as I finish setting the table. "You entered the password wrong too many times, so it locked you out. I did a password recovery and changed it again."

"I hope you made it something easy this time."

"Easier than what it was before? Your birthday?"

Dad shrugs. "I'm too old to remember my birthday."

I glare at him. "Well, now it's 12345. Think you can remember that?"

Dad scratches his head. "One . . . two . . . three . . . wait, what was next?"

I shake my head at him, but laugh a little. Dad's not great at technology. He's a bit stuck in the past. Or, as he would put it, he "appreciates the classics". And he's taught me to appreciate them too.

TIP 9

THINGS ARE CLASSIC FOR A REASON.
Don't get me wrong – I'm all about bigger, better and faster. I can't imagine a world without the internet, or Google, or online banking, or Spotify. But Dad has shown me how to appreciate the old stuff too. Music, movies and, most importantly, business. While I totally love entrepreneurs like Alexa Hirschfeld and Daniel Ek, I have learnt loads from old people like Richard Branson and Oprah Winfrey. If something is old and we still know about it today, there's a reason why it's stuck around. It's probably pretty good.

"Dane! Sash! Table. Now!" Dad shouts. "Liv! Poke time."

"I'll do it, Dad." I grab Olivia's kit and head into the lounge room. Her head is still buried in a book, and she barely acknowledges my presence as I grab her finger and pop it onto the poker. A little drop of blood bubbles up and I wipe it onto the strip.

"I was going to do it," Olivia says. "After this chapter."

"I know. But this way, you don't have to stop reading. Plus, sometimes I like to do it again, for old times' sake."

"You're weird," says Olivia, but I get a little grin from her.

As the glucose monitor does its thing, I ask, "Any guesses?"

Without looking up from her book, Olivia answers, "Um, 6.1 maybe?"

I look at the machine. "Oh, so close. But not close enough. It's 6.3. You lose!" I shut her book and lightly bop her on the head with it. "It's a 6.3!" I call to Dad.

"OK, good. Everyone. Table. Now," he calls back.

Dad finally gets us all to sit.

"Sash! Unplug."

Sash sighs dramatically and takes out her headphones. Dad serves up the fettuccine and sauce separately, measuring out Olivia's portion.

"Where's Mum?" Olivia asks, picking up a sauce-free ribbon of pasta and lowering it into her mouth.

"Where do you think?" says Sash. "Work."

"Surprise, surprise," says Dane, with a mouth full of pasta.

Dad puts down his fork. "That's enough, guys. She just texted me and she'll be home soon."

Dane slurps up his fettuccine. "Uh huh, sure."

I don't bother getting involved. We have this conversation every dinner and it always turns out the same.

Mum works at Balthazar Theatre. Before you think "cool!" – it's not. It's not all the free movies I want to see. It's not *that* kind of theatre. It's an actual theatre theatre. Where they do plays and stuff. I mean, they actually do Shakespeare plays. Have you ever seen one of them? They're long and B . . . O . . . R . . . I . . . N . . . G. She doesn't mingle with famous actors or dress up in ball gowns for opening nights. It's nothing like it is in the movies. What she does is work long shifts with early starts and late finishes. What she does is get called in all the time to cover other people. And what she does is not get paid much to do it all.

She's the Operations Manager. Which really just means she's the first to get there and last to leave. I don't think she likes it that much, either. I always ask her why she became an Operations Manager. She says she just "fell into it". I've decided I will never "fall into" a job. So I started planning and working towards my career goals at the age of six.

TIP 10

HAVE GOALS!

Think about what you want to be when you grow up, but don't pick from movies. Movies are not the real version. They get paid to make boring jobs look exciting. Look at the people around you. Read biographies (they're books about people's lives). Talk to adults. Get the real story. Pick someone you want to be like and then work for it.

So Mum misses dinner a lot. It doesn't really bother me, but I think Liv misses her.

Before Dad quit his job, Mum used to take me, Dane and Sash to the theatre all the time. It's a good place to hide kids when you can't afford a babysitter. I guess we used to like it back then. Sash spent hours in the tech booth playing with all the light and sound equipment and making stuff for us to watch. Now she just makes YouTube videos. Dane loved messing around with the sets and rigging. We played hide-and-seek and knew the best places to hide – in the props house, under the stage trapdoor, in the lighting trusses. But now that Dad's at home, we never go there any more. It's better, I guess. I get more work done now.

Jake's dinner is now completely out of his bowl and he's eating off the table. Sash has snuck one earphone back in and is watching some vlog she made of herself. Dane and Dad are yabbering on about changes they want to make to Dane's bike trailer. Although I'd never admit it to him, the trailer is pretty cool. It goes on the back of his bike when he does his flyer delivery route. Butthead sits in it with the flyers and helps Dane deliver them. Dane trains Butthead to do some pretty impressive things when he's not chasing his own tail around in circles!

We finish our family dinner (minus Mum) and Dad cleans Jake up. With the mess that he makes of himself when he eats, sometimes I think it would be easier to just strip him off and hose him down in the garden like we do to Butthead when he rolls in another dog's poo. I suggest it to Dad. Although he says no, I think he's tempted.

I clean up the table and load the dishwasher. It's probably not my turn, but most nights it's easier to just do it than argue with everyone about whose turn it is on the roster. Sash is back in her room and Dane is building something with Butthead in the lounge.

"Bring me the red piece. No, the RED piece, Butthead. That's blue," Dane says.

I stick my head in. "Why are you trying to teach him to fetch Lego?"

"Why not? No one else plays Lego with me," Dane says. "So sometimes I gotta be a little creative."

If you're feeling sorry for Dane here, don't. I've tried playing Lego with him and it's impossible. Dane's really good at building stuff and, other than passing him the pieces he needs, he barely lets you help.

"Not sure Butthead is the best playmate, though," I say. "Aren't dogs colour blind?"

"Seriously?" Dane asks, looking at Butthead holding a yellow Lego piece in his mouth.

I shrug. "That's what Google says."

I finish with the dishwasher and leave Dad to wrangle Jake as I head upstairs.

In my room, "Kids In America" by Kim Wilde is playing on my ancient laptop. It used to be Sash's and it's about seven years old so it's almost the size of my desk and weighs more than me, but it works. After spending my life as a middle child, I know there's no point in asking for anything new. Everything goes through Sash, then to Dane and then to me. I have to feel sorry for Jake. He'll probably be using this same laptop when his classmates all have robot butlers. Luckily, at the moment he's happy with a table leg to chew.

I spend the next hour or so researching stuff on the internet. I check out crowdfunding. I've heard a bit about it and want to see if I can use it to fund my next business venture. I need some cashflow because I want to buy something retro. Retro is totally in now. I open a new tab, Google "retro" and scroll through the pictures. Maybe I could get a jukebox. If I could find an original one from the 60s or 70s it would have all my favourite songs on it. Or maybe a pinball machine – I could set that up at school and collect the money that the kids pile into it. But I look at the prices and retro stuff is expensive, which brings me back to the crowdfunding. Usually being old makes things cheap, but apparently being "in" makes things expensive. Hopefully that will happen soon to my laptop.

I hear Mum's car pull up. Three, two . . . and there's Olivia's footsteps thumping downstairs. She's getting quicker every week. I look at my watch. It's 9:07pm, so she should already be asleep by now, but she always tries to stay up until Mum gets home. I listen as Mum carries her back to her room and puts her to bed. I can hear Mum's muffled voice as she reads Liv a story. Ten minutes later my door cracks open.

"Hey, Tess," Mum says. She's all dusty and her hair's a mess. She looks tired too, but she always looks tired. "All good?"

"Yeah, Mum. How was work?"

"Oh, you know, same old. Electrical problems this time. Dad said you did the dishwasher again. Thanks. But you know you can get Dane and Sash to help?"

I turn back to my laptop. "It's fine."

"Do I get a hug?"

I get up from my desk and give Mum a quick squeeze.

"So what are you working on?" she asks, nodding towards my laptop.

"A few things. I was just looking at interest rates and I think I want to transfer my no-access savings to another bank. They're at 3.64 per cent now."

Mum shakes her head at me. "Whose child ARE you?" She gives me a quick kiss. "You all good, kiddo? Need help with anything? Homework?"

I shake my head. "Homework's done, clothes are out for tomorrow and I did February's calendar and put it on the fridge. I added Liv to the green jobs like you asked."

Mum runs her hand over my hair. "Great. Almost ready for bed?"

"I have a bit more to do."

"OK. But not too late, all right? Before nine thirty. Love you."

"Me too, Mum."

She closes the door quietly and heads downstairs. I don't get a bedtime story, but I'm too old for that now anyway.

It's 9:48pm and I'm still not in bed, but Mum hasn't come up to check.

I hear Mum and Dad downstairs. I can guess what they're arguing about even before I sneak down to eavesdrop, but I do it anyway. Mum and Dad don't fight that often, but when they do, it's about one of two things: Olivia or money. It's the end of the month, so I'm guessing it's about money.

I tiptoe down the stairs and sit right on the edge of the fifth step. From here, I can see the kitchen table, but the stream of light passes just next to my leg so you can't see me from downstairs. It's not the first time I've sat here. Because Mum doesn't get home until late, I never get a chance to hear about her day. This is a good place to sit, listen in and catch up on what's going on with her.

They're at the table. Mum's eating leftover fettuccine, and Dad has papers spread out and his laptop open in front of him. He's squinting at it like it's an alien and typing painfully slowly using only two fingers.

"I know Tess said it was something really easy to remember . . ."

I roll my eyes. It's OK to do that now because nobody is watching. *Look at the top of the screen, Dad!* I wrote the new password on a label and put it just above the screen because I knew Dad would forget. *Look up!*

Mum taps the label. "Could that be it?"

Dad smiles. "Good old Tess!"

Good old Tess? *I'm ten, Dad!* He's so embarrassing.

"OK, got it open," says Dad.

"So when was the last payment? We can't owe that much again already."

Dad scrolls down on the screen. "Yeah, end of October. Sorry, it's quarterly."

Mum drops her head into her hands. "But we wanted to get Liv an insulin pump this month. And we still haven't paid last quarter's electricity bill."

"Hon, maybe we should think about me going back to work. Even just for a few days a week."

"But with Jake it would cost more to pay for nursery than the money you'd make. And someone needs to be around for Liv. It's just not worth it."

"OK, so what about at night? After you get home?"

Mum tosses the papers aside. "Yeah, great idea. Then we'll never see each other."

"I'm just trying to help," Dad says. "Don't get snarky at me."

I decide to go back to my room. I know where this argument is going and I don't need to hear it again. I turn to see Olivia standing outside her bedroom door. Her pyjamas used to be mine and they're a bit too big for her. She looks even smaller than usual.

"Are they fighting again?" she asks.

"Not really," I say, walking over to her.

"Is it me?" She looks up at me. She's chewing on her bottom lip. I don't like it when she does that. "Are they fighting about me?"

"Of course not."

"I don't believe you."

"Well, you don't have a choice," I say, putting my hand on her shoulder and steering her back into her room. "I'm your big sister, so you have to believe everything I say."

"Do you believe everything Sash says?"

"No, but that's different." I pull back her duvet. Liv crawls into bed and I tuck her in.

"Why?" she asks.

"Because Sash isn't a genius like me."

Liv laughs and I grin back at her. "Now go back to sleep."

"Mum will be in soon for poke time anyway."

"Then just pretend to be asleep," I say.

"Can you put on the diamond shoes song?" Liv asks as she snuggles her chin down below her duvet.

"Sure." I pop open the CD player on her desk. It used to be the family one, then mine and now it's Olivia's. It skipped Sash because she "wouldn't be seen dead with a CD player" and Dane because he's just not that into music. I'll never understand that. But before you go feeling sorry for Liv that she gets the crappy old CD player, it did come with an awesome CD collection. Mostly Dad's music, filtered by me. The result being that unlike Sash, who has terrible taste in music, and Dane, who has no taste, Liv is really starting to get it. As I press play and "Diamonds on the Soles of Her Shoes" begins, I couldn't be prouder that Paul Simon is her favourite.

I head out of her room and, as I pull the door closed, she calls out.

"Hey, Tess."

"Yeah."

"Am I a genius like you?"

"Yeah, you and I must have Mum's genes."

Liv giggles. "Poor Dad."

"But at least we got his taste in music."

I pull the door closed and go back to my room.

8

Not Just Another Saturday

Our street's boring. Like super boring. Nothing. EVER. Happens.

On this boring street in this boring neighbourhood live boring people with boring lives. Of course, the exception is Scotty. And it's because of him that the only interesting thing ever to happen to Wyndeman Close . . . happened.

It's Saturday morning. We've already gone through the madness of a typical Heckleston Saturday. Mum's at work. Dad's taken Dane to karate. Olivia and Jake went with him. I'm at home with Sash. Well, I assume she's somewhere

54

in the house. Being at home with Sash is like being at home with a television that doesn't work. You know it's there, but it might as well not be.

I'm in my bedroom listening to "Bad Moon Rising" by Creedence Clearwater Revival. My MP3 player is a hand-me-down from Dad and still has all his songs on it. Sash reckons she can reset it and put some of her music on it for me. Songs from "this century", she says. But I've heard the noise that comes from her room and I can't think of anything worse.

It's 10:30 and Toby's not coming over until lunchtime. I'm bored. And it's pretty hot today. I wish we had a swimming pool. My future house is so going to have a swimming pool. I go over to my window and rest my head on the cool glass. I'm hoping for some action at Scotty's, but it looks like everyone's still sleeping.

As if answering my wishes, Scotty runs into the kitchen. He's moving fast. Scotty doesn't often move fast. Through the sliding doors I can see he's got his mobile phone pressed to his ear and he's shouting. It's like watching the TV with the sound down, but he's definitely panicky because within seconds there are people running around in their pyjamas and grabbing things. Scotty's screaming at them all and pointing.

Being a naturally curious person – curious, not nosy – I really want to hear what's going on. I grab the bottom of my window and push it up, sliding it open. I still can't hear much. I think about going down to the garden, but I don't want to miss anything.

I don't know what's going on over there. Everyone's running around like their pants are on fire. Grabbing things and shoving them into bags. Hiding things. Throwing things. I can't see what any of it is but it must be important.

Then I hear it. In the distance at first, but I hear it. Sirens. Not an ambulance. Definitely police. The police NEVER come to Wyndeman Close.

Scotty hears it too.

He shouts something and even though I'm no lip-reader, I'm pretty sure it's a swear word. He runs into another room and comes out clutching a navy blue sports bag. The sirens are getting closer.

People start running in all directions. Some bolt out of the house. Scotty looks around frantically, opening cupboard doors and slamming them closed again. What's he looking for?

He runs out into the garden.

He swears again. This time I can hear it.

He looks around and then . . . he looks up at me. He pauses.

I can't move. I just kind of stare at him.

He gives me a strange smile and then throws the bag over our fence. Reaching up, he pulls himself over too.

Scotty is in our back garden.

I freeze.

I know I should get Sash or call Dad but I just can't move. Scotty grabs the bag from the grass and runs over to my treasure chest. He opens the lid, pulls out all my toys and lifts up the false bottom. Throwing the bag inside, he squishes it down. The false bottom goes back in, toys on top, lid closed and, before I can even work out what just happened, he's back over the fence and in his own garden.

The sirens are really close now. I think our boring street just became seriously un-boring. I bet all the neighbours are out in their front gardens like stunned seagulls gawking at hot chips.

But Scotty is just standing there staring at me. And I'm staring back.

The sirens are here now. I hear the screeching of car wheels. Police flood into Scotty's house, shouting. I feel like I'm watching a movie. "Another One Bites the Dust" is playing in my head.

But Scotty isn't moving. He's just looking at me. As the police approach him, he raises his hands in the air. But one hand moves to his mouth. He places his finger in front of his lips and over all the noise and craziness and theme music, I'm sure I can hear his, "Shhhh."

I don't know why. I think I know it's wrong. But just before he disappears under a pile of police officers pushing him to the ground, I look him straight in the eye . . . and nod.

$

"DAD, I'm completely serious!"

My bedroom door flies open and Sash comes storming in, her phone pinned to the side of her head. She's unplugged. Sash doesn't knock when she's unplugged. She also speaks Sash-lish, which often needs translating.

"There's like a thousand police cars." There's less than ten.

"And about a million police." I would say maybe fifteen to twenty.

"And they're totally ransacking that Scotty guy's house." They're calmly looking through the house.

"And they've got him pinned to the ground. No, wait, they're getting him up now. OMG, Dad! He's totally handcuffed. They're fully taking him to jail. You have to come home, like now." OK, all of that is pretty accurate.

"I gotta go, I'm totally missing it all."

Sash hangs up on Dad, pushes her phone through my window and starts filming. "Seriously, Tess, did you see it all from up here? Your room has the best view of his place. What happened? Did he kill someone?"

The police are asking Scotty questions. He doesn't seem to be answering them. I watch Sash as she glides across my window, getting the best angle of the action. "I don't think he killed anyone," I say. "I don't know what happened. They just all came in."

"Did you see everything? Did they have guns? Did he fight them? What happened?"

I watch Scotty as the police push him out of the kitchen. Just before he disappears into the hall he looks back up at me one more time with a look that says . . . I don't know what it says . . . but it's a knowing look. I think it says . . . "Don't say anything."

Sash squeals. "He totally just looked at us! I fully got that in the shot. I'm SO posting this. I always knew he was dodgy as."

She taps away at her screen and I move towards the door. "I'm gonna go down and take a look at the police cars."

Sash doesn't lift her head. "Yeah, I already got shots of those," she says and continues to tap. "This is gonna make the best video."

I run down the stairs to the front door and open it a crack. The whole street is out on their front lawns watching. A policeman puts his hand on Scotty's head as he pushes him into the police car.

"Tess!" Sash calls from upstairs. "Close the door and get back inside. Dad just texted. He's on his way home and he says we can't go outside till he gets back. As if we'd want to go outside with that murderer out there."

I don't bother telling Sash that I don't think Scotty is a murderer. He obviously did something bad, but I doubt he killed anyone. I can definitely think of a reason I would like to go outside, though. Out into the back garden. Just for a minute. Just to look inside my treasure chest.

Why didn't I tell someone? Tell my sister. Or when Dad got home with Jake and Dane and herded us all into the lounge like sheep – why didn't I tell him? Or even call the police and tell them? I'm sure you're all thinking "that's what I would have done".

Well, when you're from a family of five kids, sharing your stories is hard. Everyone talks at once.

When I was younger, I used to try to squeeze in here or there but eventually I gave up. And I discovered it's much more relaxing when you don't bother competing.

So the thing with Scotty, what I saw him do, I wasn't keeping it a secret. Not really. I just didn't tell anyone.

Until Toby came over, that is.

It takes ages for all the madness to settle down. Dad won't let any of us leave the house and he's been texting Mum like crazy, even though he knows she won't answer until her break. Now he's on the phone to Fara, one of Toby's mums. The funny one. She and Dad are best friends.

Fara speaks so loud I can hear her through the phone.

"I haven't seen this much action on Wyndeman Close since Butthead discovered his own tail," Fara says. She then laughs at her own joke, which she always does. Her laugh sounds like a goose honking, which makes other people laugh, which makes her think her jokes are funny . . . which most of the time they're not so much.

So now Dad's laughing too. "I know, right? I mean, we always thought something shady was going on over there, but I don't think anyone expected this."

"We have to go to the shop today. You still OK for me to bring Toby over?" Toby's mums own a print shop in Watterson called Copy Cats. It's a really cool place that designs and prints promotional material for businesses. Toby's mum Fara is the one who gave Dane his delivery job. They're open on weekends, so Toby hangs out at our place loads.

Dad looks over to me and I nod furiously. "That's a roger from Tessels!"

I groan.

Fara's laugh honks down the phone. "I could hear that groan from here. OK, I'll bring him over in about an hour. Ciao."

"Arrivederci," Dad says and hangs up the phone.

That's when I decide it's OK that I didn't tell Sash or Dad or the police about the bag. Because when you have a secret, there's one person who should ALWAYS be the first to know. And that's your best friend.

TIP 11

ALWAYS LISTEN TO YOUR BEST FRIEND'S ADVICE.

You have chosen your best friend for a reason. They are smart, they have your best interests at heart and they know what's good for you.

So you should always listen to their advice.

9

Toby's Advice

"You should tell your dad!"

I roll my eyes at Toby. "What would you know?"

"You HAVE to," he says. "A criminal, a REAL criminal put something – probably something ILLEGAL – on YOUR property. You have to tell him so he can tell the police."

I scoff. "You give the worst advice."

Toby is a good friend, but he's such a worry-wart. He's always worried that we're going to get in trouble.

"What if you get in trouble?" he says.

See!

"Why would I get in trouble? I haven't done anything. I mean, we don't even know what's in there."

"That's true," says Toby. "But he just got raided and dragged away by twenty police. I'm guessing it's not a bag of sweets."

"Fine," I say. "How's this for a plan? We go have a look. Together. See what it is. And THEN we decide what to do. Deal?"

Toby thinks about it for a bit, but I'm pretty sure that, under the good-kid act, he really wants to see what's in there as much as I do.

"Deal!" he says.

Getting outside to take a look is harder than we expect. The police are at Scotty's place for ages, and we don't want to go look while they're still there. For one thing, they might ask us if we saw anything, and although I don't want to go running to Dad before I even know what Scotty hid, I also don't want to lie to the police. I know you may think I'm not the best, most honest, well-behaved kid on the planet, but I don't like to lie. Really I don't. I don't always tell the truth, the whole truth and nothing but the truth, but generally I try not to lie either.

So Toby and I hang around in the house waiting for them all to leave. It's not easy. It's like when your Christmas present arrives from your grandma a week before Christmas and just sits under the tree staring at you. Begging to be opened. But you have to wait. Even though you can almost hear it calling to you.

Come on, Tess. Open me. Just tear off a little corner and take a peek. No one will know.

Well, it's like that.

So Toby and I are faking a game of Hungry Hungry Hippos. I would have thought that would be a dead giveaway that we're up to something – I mean, no one in our house (or probably on the planet) has played that game for years. But it means we can look occupied whilst being focused on something else.

Toby and I tap mindlessly on the hippos as they barely eat any of the little white balls.

"You guys suck at that game," says Dane. "You do know you're supposed to be eating the balls?"

"Uh huh," I say.

"Butthead, get the game!" Dane demands. Butt-head trots over and grabs the Hungry Hippo game between his teeth, dragging it back over to Dane.

"Hey!" I say, more annoyed that he's stolen our cover than interrupted our fake game.

"See! He can fetch anything he's told to, can't you?" Dane says, giving Butthead a rub under the chin. "He's a clever dog. Aren't you, Butty?"

As if on cue, Butthead growls defensively at the blue hippo. He crouches down, preparing for a plastic hippo attack at any second.

"Oh yeah, total dog genius!" I scoff, snapping the hippo at Butthead as he cowers in fear.

"Shut up!" Dane grabs Butthead and hauls him off.

Finally everything quietens down. The police are thinning out, Dad has stopped pacing and the Hecklestons are all back to their usual Saturday activities.

"Dad," I call from the lounge. "Toby and I are going out to the garden, ок?"

"ок," he calls back. "Can you send Liv in for her insulin first?"

"But Dad, she's upstairs!" By now I'm itching to get outside so bad it feels like that time I commando crawled through a thistle patch when we were spying on Jacinta Drew. Totally wasn't worth the ten dollars Indrup Patel paid us.

"Now, Tess!"

I groan. Olivia's a cool kid, but she often messes up my schedule. Dane and Sash used to help with Liv, but now that they're in high school it's my job, because Liv and I are still at the same school.

"Wait here," I say to Toby.

I run upstairs and push open Olivia's door without knocking – that rule only applies when it's an older sibling's room.

Liv is sitting cross-legged on the floor, and swipes something under her skirt when I come in. I pause.

"Dad says to go downstairs for your shot," I say slowly, my detective brain analysing the scene. Olivia nods far too enthusiastically for insulin time.

"OK. Yep, I'll be down in a minute," she says.

I examine her face as a red colour creeps up her neck. Liv has always been the worst liar.

"What's under your dress?"

"Nothing," she says quietly.

"Olivia?" I give her the "big sister" look. It gets her every time. She sighs and pulls out a handful of sweets.

My mouth drops open. "Liv! Are you crazy?"

"I wasn't going to eat them!"

"Yeah right. You were just going to play draughts with them? Where did you even get those?"

"From school," Olivia says, dropping her head.

"But Ms Jensen knows with your diabetes you can't –"

"I won them. In the playground. The kids were having a jumping competition. I can jump really far, you know?"

I walk over to Olivia and take the sweets from her. "You have diabetes. You know you can't sneak sweets." I look at her. Most seven-year-olds would throw a tantrum right now, but Olivia just twists the hem of her skirt.

"I know, Tess," she says. "I just wanted to play with the other kids. Even if I couldn't really have the prize." She stands up and heads downstairs to Dad. She stops halfway and turns to me.

"You and Toby can eat them if you want. They're the sour ones. The kids at school love them."

I watch her as she disappears into the kitchen. It's nice of her, I guess, and normally I'm a big fan of sour sweets, but right now I have just one thing on my mind.

"Toby! Back garden. Now."

10

The Treasure Chest

Toby and I are standing next to my treasure chest, peering in. Stuffed inside is a dark blue sports bag. It's pretty full and only just fits in.

"What if it's a bomb?" Toby says.

"C'mon, Toby. It's not going to be a bomb. Why would he want to hide a bomb in my back garden?"

My mind starts racing.

"You open it, Toby."

"What? Why me?"

I shrug. "In case it's a bomb."

Toby shakes his head. "You're the worst best friend ever, you know? You open it."

My curiosity outweighs my fear, so I reach inside and find the zip. Toby and I lean in further and hold our breaths. I slowly tug on the tag as it slides across the zipper teeth. A small opening grows, just enough to . . .

"TESS!"

Toby and I spin around, instinctively shutting the lid and sitting on top. Dad's standing at the door wearing his favourite "Keep Calm and Cook" apron. His eyes narrow as he stares at us. "All right, what are you two up to?"

"Nothing, Dad," I say in my best innocent voice. "Just looking through my stuff, deciding what to play with." It's not really a lie. We *were* looking and we *might* play with it, if it turns out to be a bag full of Lego.

"OK, well, I don't believe that at all but I'm feeding Liv and Jake. Can you guys come in for some lunch, please?"

"Sure, Dad. Be in in a sec."

"Five minutes," Dad says. "I've made a quiche and I don't want it getting cold."

"OK."

Dad heads inside and Toby and I turn back to the bag. No more messing about. I yank the zip back.

Wads of money burst out of the opening. Toby and I stare at the cash. We don't say a word. I'm not even sure we're breathing.

Toby finally whispers, "How much do you think is there?"

"Hundreds. Thousands maybe."

Toby turns to me. "Millions?"

I nod. Excitement bubbles in my chest.

"But we can't keep it, can we?" Toby asks.

"I don't see why not. Scotty gave it to me. It's in my treasure chest and possession is nine-tenths of the law."

"What does that even mean?" Toby whispers.

"It means . . . I just became a millionaire."

"Tess! Toby! Inside, now!" Dad calls through the kitchen window.

I close the lid of the box, face Toby and raise my finger to my lips. "Shhhh."

$

We stuff our lunch down and then the two of us drag the bag upstairs. Jake's having a post-lunch meltdown, so Dad doesn't even notice.

Now Toby and I sit on the floor of my bedroom surrounded by cash. Cat Stevens' "Wild World" is playing, but for the first time ever, Toby isn't complaining about my ancient taste in music.

My eyes sting a little as I stare at the money sitting in neat stacks around us. I think I might have stopped blinking.

"Are you sure, Toby?" I say. We've counted the money twice since lunch. It's taken most of the afternoon, but we had to be sure.

Toby looks at the calculator again and nods. "Yup. One million dollars."

There's another minute of silence as it sinks in. After all the hard work, the planning, the ideas that failed and picking ourselves back up again . . . who would have thought that *this* was how we'd become rich. It doesn't look quite how I'd imagined. Not like the movies. Not neat little piles of crisp one-hundred-dollar notes. This money is made up of random notes – lots of hundreds and fifties, a few twenties, mostly older notes. It's been stuffed into the bag, all crumpled and used. Also, somehow it doesn't look enough to be a million dollars. I imagined a million dollars would be enough to swim in, but this fits snugly into the gym bag.

"So what now?" I ask Toby.

"In the movies, they toss it into the air and let it rain down on them. Or they throw it at each other in a joyous money fight."

I pick up a wad of cash and throw it at Toby's head. It bounces off with a dull thud and lands on the ground next to him.

"Ow!"

I raise my eyebrows at him. "Next idea?"

Toby rubs his head and glares at me. "I don't think we can keep it, Tess."

I jump to my feet. "What are you talking about? This is what we've been dreaming of since we were six! We have enough money to do everything we've ever wanted, and you want to do what? Give it back?"

"It's not right. We didn't earn it."

"Earn it? Look, we've done nothing but work for years while other kids played Xbox, and this is our reward. You think people only get what they earn in this world? Look at my mum. She works like crazy and has nothing, and then people just win the lottery by taking ten seconds to buy a ticket and become instant millionaires. This is OUR lottery!"

"I dunno. It just doesn't seem right."

I sit down next to him. "We didn't steal this money. Scotty gave it to me."

"He didn't GIVE it to you. He hid it in your garden while he was getting arrested by the police. And what about when he comes back for it?" Toby's head tilts to the side and he bites down on the inside of his cheek. I know this look. It's a bad sign. He's not on board.

"He's not coming back. He got dragged off by a hundred police. He's going to jail . . . for a very long time. You think he can do anything with a million dollars in jail? Think what WE can do with it. We could pay to get that old printer at your mums' shop upgraded. Or hire an assistant so they don't have to work on Sundays. We could fund that guide dog training programme you wanted to do at school that they said no to. Or do the overnight stay at the zoo."

Toby shifts on the floor and his back straightens up a little. I know this sign. I've seen it before. It means he's coming round, he's being swayed. I need to talk fast and drown out his sense of logic. It's what I do best.

"We could fix Fara's car so it doesn't pollute the air with that weird purple smoke. Or even better, get her a new car! We could buy Liv that pump she needs. Or . . ."

I can see it, I nearly have him. I need to seal the deal.

"You know what we could do with this, Toby?" I pause for effect. "We could fund *everybody* on Watsi."

Toby's head snaps up. That's it. I've got him.

"OK," Toby says slowly. "If you mean it – if you want to use the money to do good – I'm in. But we need a plan."

I nod, smiling. "Yes, we'll use it to do good. I'll pack up the money. You start making the list. Better make a Toby column and a Tess column so we can do a little of everything."

I'm thinking I'll sneak my spa bath and the school waterslide in there somewhere.

Toby's eyes are wide and excited now. He's *so* on board. "Awesome!" he grins. "I love lists!" He goes to jump up, but I stop him.

"Just before we do . . ." I grab a wad of cash, take off the rubber band and switch the track on the MP3 player, cranking up the volume. As "Don't Stop Believin'" booms out of my crackling speakers, I toss the money into the air. Toby and I laugh as the notes rain down on us.

"And that, my friend, is how they do it in the movies!"

11

The Schoolyard Millionaire

TIP 12

LIVE A LITTLE.

It's hard to be a kid these days. There's a lot of
pressure to succeed, to focus on schoolwork,
to be good, to be smart, to be sensible.
So, every now and then, just take a moment to
enjoy life. 'Cos one day soon you'll be an adult.
And then the fun is all over.

My life has never felt more like a movie than
this moment. And it's in slow motion for sure.

The soundtrack's gotta be "For the Love of Money" by The O'Jays. I love a bit of 70s funk. We round the corner of the school corridor just as the high hat kicks in. Toby and I both have sunglasses on indoors, because if you've watched enough movies or American reality TV, you know that's what the rich people do. We strut down the school corridor, tossing strawberry-and-cream lollipops to our adoring fans, who cheer us on all the way from our classroom.

Toby and I spent a productive Sunday writing and rewriting our lists, calculating our costs, stocking up on supplies and planning our change of status in the schoolyard. So by Monday lunch, we own that school.

The lollipops are my idea. I like to reward my admirers. The Pitch Desk is Toby's idea. He wants to start using the money to do good straightaway. I guess to balance out the lollipops.

Toby printed the flyers at his mums' print shop and we paid a Year Three to hand them out to all the kids. Toby did a great job of the flyers – he's really good at Photoshop. He does his family's Christmas cards every year, and manages to Photoshop him and his mums in a different exotic location each time.

Anyway, the flyers look great. They have money notes and dollar signs all around the border and read:

THE PITCH DESK – TOP SECRET!

Do you have a great idea but no cash to do it?

Pocket money just not cutting it?

Then come to THE PITCH DESK!

You have one minute to pitch your idea and tell us how much money you need to make it happen.
If we deem it worthy, the money is yours.
No strings attached.

Lunchtime – Monday – the back field banks.

NO ADULTS ALLOWED!

PS Preference will be given to charitable ideas.

Toby made me put in that last bit, but I made him shrink it down to size six font. We're good at compromising.

We strut down to the back field with our horde of followers. This is what it feels like to be rich and famous. I like it. The back field banks are technically out of bounds. But there's so much undergrowth that they're hidden from the sight of the teachers unless they actually make the effort to walk all the way down there . . . which they never do. But there's still an old picnic bench there, and Toby has set it up between the last two classes. He organises the kids into a line and I take my seat at the desk. One by one they approach.

"State your name, year, amount needed and idea," Toby explains with a newfound authority that I think he's quite enjoying. "You have one minute . . . GO!"

"Craig Martin, Year Six, thirty-nine dollars." The kid in front of us seems nervous, even though he's older than we are. "There's this new Future Extinction game for PlayStation, and Mum won't let me get it, and it's got like robot dinosaurs, and you're this guy and you have to go through this forest and shoot all these—"

I raise my hand to stop him. I stand up and address all the kids in line.

"Let me make this very clear: I will not be giving anyone money to buy video games." About ten kids groan and leave the line, including Craig. "This is an opportunity for entrepreneurs, guys. Great ideas. Ideas that will change the world. Original ideas." I sit back down and shake my head at Toby. "Seriously, kids these days . . . NEXT!"

"Valentina Arizti, Year Three. My birthday is coming up, and I want to rent out the zoo and invite all my friends so we can pat the bears and ride the elephants."

I can't help but smile. She reminds me of Liv. "Are you sure you want to pat the bears?"

Valentina thinks about it. "How about the koalas?"

"Better. How much do you think you'll need?"

"Um, maybe a hundred dollars?"

Toby takes over. "Tell you what. How about we give you three hundred dollars, and you rent out the animal shelter instead? You can pat all the animals you want to AND the money goes to a good cause."

She thinks about it for a moment, then nods excitedly. "And you guys can come too, OK?"

"Deal!" says Toby and hands the girl three one-hundred-dollar notes.

"Whoa! Thanks," she says as she walks off. The sight of cash sends a buzz down the line and things really kick off.

"Anishka Batan, Year Five, one thousand dollars. I wanna rent Tim Cahill for the day to play on our football team so we can finally beat the Red Hill Raiders. They've been on top of the ladder for way too long and it's not fair."

"But hiring a professional football player is fair?" Toby asks.

"I dunno. I just wanna win."

"Next!" I call. I've never been a big sports fan anyway.

"Jasper Zabikas, Year Two, one hundred dollars."

"OK, Jasper, let's hear it," I say.

"I want to buy a bunch of LED lights so I can make a big flashing sign for my dog so he knows where to do his business, 'cos my neighbour says if he does it on his lawn one more time, he's going to get him taken care of. And I don't think it's the good kind of taken care of like Mum does for me when I'm sick."

"What makes you think that your dog will follow the flashing sign?" I ask.

"Well, at Christmas time he always poos under the Christmas tree, so I'm just hoping he likes the lights."

I shrug. "Worth a try, right?" Toby hands him one hundred dollars. "Next."

"Casey Wu, Year Six, three hundred dollars."

Casey is the prankster at school, so I'm pretty keen to hear what she has planned.

"I want to buy a bunch of alarm clocks and set them all a minute apart, then sneak in before school assembly and tape them to the bottom of all the chairs. Then, during assembly, they'll go off one by one and drive the teachers mad trying to work out where the noise is coming from. I'm going to get one that makes a chicken noise and set that to go off last, and that'll go under Mrs Keiren's chair."

I look at Toby and he shakes his head. "Pleeeeease!" I beg.

"No," he says. "You promised we weren't going to waste the money."

"This isn't a waste!" I say. "This would be hilarious, and laughter brings happiness to the world and—"

"No!"

"Sorry," I say to Casey but, as she walks off, I decide I'll try and slip her a little cash later. I really want to see that chicken clock under Mrs Kieren's butt.

By the time the school bell rings, we've only given away six hundred dollars. "I'm a bit disappointed," I say to Toby as we pack up our things. "I would have thought kids were a bit more ingenious than that."

Toby stops and glares at me. "That's not what's disappointing, Tess. Not one kid had an idea that would help other people. It was all about them. We have a million dollars. That can change people's lives – people who really need it – and we're giving it away to kids to buy toys."

"Hey!" I say, grabbing our stuff and heading back towards the classrooms. "We didn't give anyone money to buy toys. Except maybe that motorised scooter for Micah, but that was to improve the efficiency of his can collecting. I can't resist efficiency improvement."

"I'm serious. I only agreed to keep the money because you said we'd do good with it, and so far we've done nothing but waste it on pointless ideas and strawberry-and-cream lollipops. What happened to helping our families? Or the poor? Or the sick?"

"I tried to donate on Watsi, but you need a credit card. You need a credit card for everything we want to do. It's not that easy."

Toby stops and turns on me. He's doing the Chihuahua thing and starting to shake a little. Not 'cos he's scared – he also does it when he's angry.

"I know you, Tess. I know you can do anything you put your mind to. So you need to figure out a way for us to use this money to help people, or else . . ."

My jaw tightens. "Or else what? You'll dob on me?"

"I shouldn't have to threaten you. You should just know what the right thing to do is. And I know you do."

And with that, Toby storms off. The second bell rings but I wait until Toby's inside before I head in. I don't want him to think I'm following him to apologise. My neck has gone all hot and prickly. It always does that when I'm furious.

TIP 13

UNDERSTAND YOUR FEELINGS.
Sometimes you're angry, sometimes you're sad, and all of it's OK. The key is to know why. Sometimes you think you're angry at someone for one reason, but really it's another. Take the time to work it out.

I feel furious with Toby because he said he'd dob me in. Because he's supposed to be my best friend. Because it's not my fault none of the other kids had good ideas. But mostly I'm furious because he's right.

Toby's in his advanced classes after lunch so I don't see him until afternoon break. I'm leaning against the side gate near the top field when he walks up and leans next to me.

"Still angry?" he asks.

"Nah," I say. "Two hours of Mr Deery and boring history is enough to defuse anyone's anger."

Toby laughs. "Defuse? Your Google word of the day?"

"Nah. My Google word of the day is concede."

"Please use it in a sentence."

"I concede that you may have been right."

Toby turns to me and smiles. "Look, I completely agree that we should enjoy the money and have fun, but it's wrong to get this opportunity and not do something good with it, that's all. So let's just find a balance. Deal?"

I shake his hand. "Deal. Oh, and can you pay him?"

Toby spins around to see a guy in overalls walking towards us.

"That'll be three hundred and fifty dollars, thanks, miss. I'll be back at half past three to pack it up," the man says. Toby looks at me questioningly.

"Just pay him and I'll show you," I say. Toby hands the man the cash and we walk around to the top field. A bouncy castle is set up behind the upper years' playground. Kids are going bananas, running everywhere, jumping, tumbling, laughing. Even Toby must see that this is doing some good.

He chuckles. "Awesome!"

I put my arm round his shoulder. "So how about we let everyone have a bit of fun, and tomorrow we can start working out how to do some good?"

"Sounds perfect."

I reach into my bag and toss some lollipops at the kids waiting to go on. One kid I don't recognise calls out, "Three cheers for Tess!" The crowd responds with, "Hip, hip, hooray!" This feels good. This is exactly how I imagined it.

"All right, Tobes, can you keep an eye on things here? I'll see you in class."

"Where are you going?" he asks.

"I ordered a coffee and doughnut cart for the staffroom. Gotta go pay the guy."

Toby can't hide his look of surprise. "For the teachers? That's very nice of you. Which is weird."

"Hey! I can be nice. You know, it's the least they deserve for putting up with me for the last five years."

Toby puts his hand on my shoulder. "Aw, look at you growing a heart! That's very thoughtful of you, Tess."

I swat his hand off. "Mostly I'm hoping it will keep them busy for a little bit before someone spots the castle."

Toby shakes his head. "Nice try, Tess, but too late – I saw your soft side."

I choose to ignore him.

"Coffee and doughnuts will definitely keep the teachers away from the playground, but you don't think they might wonder where it all came from?" Toby asks.

"Oh, they'll know where it came from. 'The Parents of Watterson Primary' organised it, complete with a card thanking them for all their hard work and dedication to the future citizens of Watterson." I grin at Toby and he laughs.

"You are unbelievable, Tess!"

"Thanks. Gotta go."

I turn to leave when I feel a tug on my shirt.

"Did you do this, Tess?" Olivia asks, her wide eyes staring up at me.

"Sure did."

"But how?" Olivia looks around, confused. "The castle. The sweets. Do Mum and Dad know?"

"Ah no, they don't, Liv, and let's just keep it between us, OK? Just for now. If you can keep it a secret, then I'll be able to help Mum and Dad with all the bills and stuff."

"But where did you get the money?"

I pat her on the head. "Don't you worry about that. Do you trust me?"

"Of course," Olivia says.

"Good. So go enjoy it."

"I didn't, um . . . OK," Olivia says, rubbing her eyes.

"You OK, Liv?" I ask.

"Yeah," she says. "I'm just . . . I don't know where to start."

I thrust my hands dramatically in the air. "Do it all!"

I give Liv a little shove towards the fun and walk away. Behind me I hear her say to her friend, "That's my big sister!"

I smile to myself and toss a last handful of strawberry-and-cream lollipops over my shoulder to my adoring fans as the chanting of my name fades into the distance. Cue some song like "Simply the Best" as I head to the staffroom.

12

Not So Fast

Toby and I walk through Brennan Park after school. Our parents have FINALLY agreed to let us walk home from school as long as we're together. We always go through Brennan Park because it keeps us away from the road, which makes the parents happy, and it's a good place to chat about our business ideas without fear of someone overhearing. Toby also likes to drop a coin or two in a hat somewhere in the park.

"I can live without money, but I cannot live without love!"

Kooky Kathy is strumming her guitar and singing something that sounds more like a cat having its tail pulled than an actual song.

"Said the girl who played Dorothy, who fell from above."

Kooky Kathy is a Watterson icon. Everybody knows her. Mum used to go to school with Kathy, so I'm not sure when she started living in the park, but she's been there for as long as I can remember. She has wild dark hair that's sort of turning grey and has coloured bits in it. It also has other things in it, and she smells a little like that sandwich I forgot in my schoolbag for three months. She plays her guitar and invents songs that make no sense. She shouts random (although complimentary) things at passers-by and feeds the possums in the park, much to the annoyance of the Council. Oh yeah, and Toby thinks she's great. Honestly, he's a real worry sometimes.

Toby heads towards her, digging in his pockets for some coins. I hang back. That three-month-old sandwich smell is not my favourite.

"Hi, Kathy," Toby says as he throws a few coins in her beanie lying in the dirt. Recognition passes through her dreamy stare as she looks up at Toby.

"Elvis!" she calls. "Dance for me!" She furiously strums an out of tune rendition of "Blue Suede

Shoes" as Toby laughs and shakes his knees back and forth with his hands flailing in the air. He looks ridiculous. I mean, when Elvis did it, it looked silly enough, but Kooky Kathy and Toby's duet looks like a talent show for the highly untalented.

"Toby! Can we go?" I fold my arms and stare at him under my eyebrows.

"Ooohhh, your friend isn't happy, little Elvis," Kathy says. "Maybe we should fix that."

She starts to play "Don't Worry Be Happy", singing the words at the top of her scratchy voice. It's actually a great song but this version is just annoying. Toby thinks it's hilarious and joins in.

"Well, I'm going," I say and turn to leave. "You can . . . EEEEKKKK!"

A huge rat-like creature runs straight up my leg. I completely freak out, thrashing my arms and kicking my legs. I finally manage to shake it off. It hits the ground, scampers over to Kooky Kathy and climbs up onto her shoulder. Kathy laughs hysterically and Toby covers his mouth, knowing if he joins in I'll kill him.

"Her dancing is almost as good as yours, Elvis!" Kathy says.

"What is that thing?!" I yell in disgust, wiping off the rat-creature germs I can feel crawling their way all over me.

"This is Mr Piddles," Kooky Kathy says with pride. "The smartest ferret in all the world."

"Try the grossest," I mumble under my breath.

"Careful there, kiddo," warns Kathy. "Mr Piddles is my people."

"Your people?"

"Nothing is worth anything if you can't share it with your people. Everyone's gotta have their people," says Kathy. "Even if their people is a ferret."

"Seriously, Tess," says Toby. "You should see what he can do. Show her, Kathy."

Kathy lifts the furry creature off her shoulder and puts him on the ground. "Go scavenge," she says and the animal darts off, running up the side of a rubbish bin and disappearing inside.

"Oh wow," I say, rolling my eyes. "A rat that goes into rubbish bins. Amazing."

"Wait for it!" Toby says with a smile.

After a minute, Mr Piddles' little head pops up over the edge of the bin. He's got something in his mouth as he scurries back to Kooky Kathy. She reaches down and takes the object, switching it for a small piece of bread. She holds it up to us.

"Mr Piddles is a treasure hunter," she says with a proud grin. In her hand is a one-dollar coin.

"Kathy has trained him to collect valuable things," explains Toby. "He found her a FitBit the other day." Toby points to the black rubber bracelet on Kathy's wrist. "How cool is that?"

"A FitBit? Yes, very useful for Kathy, I'm sure," I say sarcastically.

Although I would never admit it out loud, I'm actually pretty impressed. A ferret after my own heart.

TIP 14

DON'T JUDGE A FERRET BY ITS RAT-LIKE APPEARANCE. OR A BOOK BY ITS COVER, OR WHATEVER.
You've heard this one before, and it's pretty hard not to do. I mean, how else are we supposed to judge people/ferrets when we

first meet them? But just be aware, the more
you rely on appearances or first impressions,
the more wrong you'll be.

I start to imagine a whole army of trained
ferrets that I could send out over the city to fetch
me riches. Then I remember . . . I ALREADY
HAVE RICHES.

"Come on, Toby, we have to go." I grab his arm
and pull him away. "We have *things to do*, remember."

"OK. See ya, Kathy." He turns to wave goodbye
but Kathy's already back on her guitar, singing
something unrecognisable to the trees.

"Why do you talk to her?" I whisper to Toby.
"She's so weird."

Toby smiles. "You're weird and I talk to you."

I grab his T-shirt and practically drag him the
rest of the way through Brennan Park.

As we emerge from the park we hear a familiar
bang and see a cloud of purple smoke moving

down the road. This is Fara's car arriving – we call it The Beast.

"Where's 'get your mum a new car' on the to-do list?" I ask Toby.

He looks at his notebook. "Sixth."

"Move it up," I say as the baby-poo brown station wagon screeches to a halt in front of us. "Fara, you guys said we could walk if . . ." I begin, but Fara leans out the window.

"Get in, guys. Olivia's in hospital."

Toby and I throw our school bags in and clamber into the back seat.

"What happened?" I ask, immediately forgetting I promised myself I'd never be seen dead riding in this car again.

"Is she ok?" Toby asks. He's starting to shake. Olivia is as much a little sister to him as she is to me.

"Is it a low?" I'm almost pleading at this stage.

"I don't know, guys," Fara says apologetically. "Your dad just asked me to come get you, Tess. I'm sure they'll tell you everything when we get there."

We ride the rest of the way in silence, except for the occasional splutter or pop from The Beast.

Toby holds my hand, and I don't think I've ever been so grateful to have him next to me.

I push through the double doors at the hospital. They're so heavy. I've seen scenes like this in the movies, where they rush up to the desk and demand which room so-and-so is in, then dramatically charge their way through doctors to get there. But the hospital makes me feel very small. And afraid. I decide I might just let Fara take the lead on this one. As she moves over to the desk, I see Dane and Sash. Sash is unplugged. She also has her arm round Dane. This is not good.

I run to them. They both stand and give me a big hug. This is really not good. I don't remember the last time we hugged. Toby runs over and joins in. I just rest there for a moment. It feels warm, and I feel sort of hidden from everything. Finally Sash lets go.

"Is she OK?" I say, unsure that I actually want to know the answer.

"Not really," says Sash. Dane looks at his feet. We all feel responsible. One of us wasn't looking out for her. Or all of us.

"She's sleeping now," says Dane. "But it was bad, Tess. Her numbers were crazy. She must have skipped her insulin."

"And Dad says she ate something she shouldn't have." Sash looks like she's about to cry. "They bought her here in an ambulance. I've never seen Mum and Dad so scared."

My tummy feels like when you go on a roller-coaster. I need to see her. Fara comes over to us.

"Can I see Liv?" I ask Fara. "Please?"

"I'm sure that will be fine, hon. She's just up there in room fourteen. Your mum and dad are with her." She runs her hand over my head and gives me a squeeze. "I have to call your ma, Tobes. She has Jake and I want to keep her updated. You guys OK?"

We all nod silently. I head towards room fourteen.

"Tess." Toby hovers behind. "You want me to come with you?"

I shake my head. "No, it's OK."

"She'll be all right, Tess."

I nod, unconvinced, and head for the thick door of Olivia's room.

I look through the small glass window. It's sort of blurry, but I can make out the shapes of Mum and Dad next to a bed in the far corner. I guess the small lump in the bed is my little sister. Suddenly, the last thing I want to do is open that door. But I push on it anyway.

A cream curtain hangs around the bed, and I walk quietly towards the edge. Mum and Dad are talking. Olivia is asleep. She looks so little in that big hospital bed. There are machines and tubes and a soft beep that doesn't stop. Her skinny arms lie on a mint-green blanket that looks like it's been washed too many times. I make a note to myself to bring her *Alice in Wonderland* blanket next time. I scrub that thought. She'll be home tomorrow, for sure.

I hover just behind the curtain. It reminds me of all those nights sitting on the stairs listening to my parents, just behind the stream of light. I can hear Mum talking.

"What was she thinking? She knows what she's supposed to do. Did you do her numbers before school?"

"Of course I did," Dad says, remaining calm.

"Then what went wrong?"

"We think she was lying about her numbers at school. And at lunch she told Ms Jensen that Tess already did her insulin." Dad puts his hand on Mum's knee but she brushes it off.

"What? Why would she do that? Someone is supposed to be monitoring this. She's only seven." Mum stands up. "If we had bought her that pump, this wouldn't have happened."

Dad runs his hand through what's left of his hair. "Please don't start this again. You think I don't want to get her the pump? We're getting there. We should have enough in a couple of months."

"Well, that seems a little late right now, don't you think?" Mum looks to Olivia, realising she's raised her voice. She sits back down. "How did she get her hands on these and why would she eat them? She knows better than that."

Mum holds something in her hand, but I can't see what it is. I edge closer.

"I'm not sure," Dad says, taking whatever it is out of her hand. "But she's a kid, and sometimes

I guess she just wants to be like all the other kids." Dad puts the thing on the bedside table and I can see what it is.

A strawberry-and-cream lollipop.

It's my fault.

I can't stop the whimper that comes from somewhere deep inside me and Mum and Dad spin round.

"Tess!" Dad jumps to his feet and gives me a hug. "Come see your sister. She'd love to know you're here."

I walk over to the bed and take Liv's hand. It's cold and floppy. It scares me. "Is she gonna be OK?" I ask Dad.

He puts his hand on my shoulder. "She'll be fine."

I look to Mum for confirmation.

"They're monitoring and correcting her levels and they'll keep her here for a bit."

"Is it DKA?" I ask.

Dad takes my hand. "Tess, I really wish you wouldn't Google Liv's diabetes. She's going to be fine. It was a bit of a scare for all of us, but we just have to be more careful and make sure she's doing the right thing and staying away from the wrong things."

I look over at the lollipop on the table and the rollercoaster tummy feeling hits again.

A doctor in a crisp white coat walks in and my parents leave me with Liv while they talk to him. I push her fringe back off her forehead and whisper to her.

"I'm so sorry, Liv. I should have been checking you were OK instead of hiring bouncy castles. Please be all right. I promise I'll be a better sister, I'll keep you out of trouble, if you can just be all right. And I'm so sorry about the lollipops."

Mum and Dad walk back in with the doctor and I give Liv a quick kiss on the forehead. "Love you, sis," I whisper and step away from the bed.

"The doctor just needs to check on Olivia," Dad says. I nod and back away from them.

"I'll wait outside with the others."

13

Wake-up Call

TIP 15

DON'T BE AN IDIOT. NO ONE LIKES AN IDIOT.

Sometimes you'll do stupid things in life.
It's inevitable – that means it's gonna happen.
But doing stupid things doesn't make you an
idiot. You become an idiot when you realise what
you're doing is stupid and you don't change.

I walk out of Olivia's hospital room in a sort of
daze. It's my fault she's in there. Realising that feels

like someone punching me in the gut. A punch well deserved.

"You OK?" Toby's standing next to me but I don't answer. I feel ashamed and stupid and guilty, all mixed up in one horrible feeling.

"Show me the list," I say and hold my hand out to Toby.

"Tess, is this the time to . . ."

"Now." Toby hands me the list and I look at it. The more I look at it, the more ashamed I feel. I tear the piece of paper away from the notebook spiral and screw it up. "We need a new list." Toby just nods. I look around the hospital waiting room. It's a sad place. Everyone looks worried about something. There are posters everywhere about diseases and medicine. One poster catches my eye. It's got a little girl on it. She looks a bit like Olivia. At the bottom, it reads: "You can help. Donate today."

"How much do you have on you right now?"

Toby rifles through his school bag. "Maybe about a thousand."

"Give it to me."

Toby looks around. "But, Tess . . ."

"Give it to me."

He hands me a wad of notes and I move over to a table under the poster. On it is a clear plastic box with a slit in the top. It's about a quarter full of coins. I start stuffing the notes in. The slit is small so I can only fit a couple at a time but I jam them in as fast as I can. I can feel my breathing getting quicker as I cram the notes inside. My eyes are starting to sting and getting a bit blurry.

"Tess." I hear Toby but he sounds far away and I ignore him. I keep stuffing frantically.

"Tess!" Toby puts his hand on mine to stop me. I look at him. I'm trying my best not to cry, but I'm not sure it's working. "It will be easier if we fold them," Toby says. I nod. Together we fold the notes and slide them in until the box is full. We're trying to get the last few in when there's a voice behind us.

"Hey! What are you two doing?"

We turn to see a nurse standing with his hands on his hips. Toby and I are holding the last of the notes.

"Did you take those out of that box?" The nurse looks angry.

"No," I say. "We're putting them in."

He comes over and snatches the notes out of our hands. "There's almost a hundred dollars here," he says. "You're trying to tell me you two kids have a spare hundred dollars to donate? Get out of here before I find your parents." The nurse stuffs the last of our notes in the box and we run off without arguing.

"There you are," says Fara, stopping us in our tracks. "Tess, I told your parents you can stay with us for a bit. Jake's going to stay with us too. Your mum and dad need to be here with Liv. Is that OK with you?"

I nod. It actually is OK with me. Toby and I have a lot of work to do, and it will be easier without my parents around. I grab my stuff and follow Fara out to The Beast.

"I feel like there's a plan hatching in there," says Toby, tapping on my head. "You're way too quiet."

"Yep," I say.

"So have our plans for the money changed?" he asks.

"Everything's changed, Toby. Everything."

The next day at school there are no sunglasses indoors. There's no slow-motion walking down the school corridor. There's no theme music. And there are definitely no strawberry-and-cream lollipops. What there is . . . is a new list. Toby and I sat up late last night making it, and I've gotta say, when I look at it I feel a whole lot better than I did last time. The kids at school seem disappointed that there are no grand gestures of wealth from me today, but I don't really care. I just want to get through the day and go see Liv.

Like it always does when you've got better things to do, the day drags by. But finally the last bell rings, and I meet Toby at his locker.

"Got the cash?" I ask. Toby pats his backpack and nods. "List?"

"Check!" he says.

We sound pretty professional now. Kind of movie-like.

As we head out the doors to the school, I turn to Toby. "Maybe we should have kept the sunglasses. It'd be so *Blues Brothers* right now if we had them."

"Seriously? *The Blues Brothers*?" Toby shakes his head. "Not cool, Tess. So not cool."

TIP 16

THE BLUES BROTHERS MOVIE IS COOL.

I don't know if your parents will let you watch it, because it has some bad words and stuff, but this movie is brilliant! It was made way back when my parents were kids, but give it a go. It's a kind of Robin Hood story about two brothers who need money to help save the orphanage they grew up in. They're not really good guys – they make a lot of mistakes along the way and get in loads of trouble, but they mean well. Sound familiar?

Fara and The Beast are waiting outside for us, purple smoke choking the other kids waiting for pick-up. I give Toby my best apologetic look. We had to move "replacement of The Beast" down on the list in the redraft.

Toby shakes his head. "I don't care, Tess. Really. It kind of suits Mum anyway."

Fara leaps out of the car and bounds over to us, crushing us in a bear hug. "How you doing, guys? You OK, Tess?"

I would nod but my head is currently being crushed in her armpit. She releases us both from her grip. "OK, so your ma has got the print shop under control, Toby, so I can run you guys over to the hospital. I have to do some shopping, so if it's cool I'll just dump you there for about forty-five minutes and then come grab you again?"

We both nod. "Sounds great, Fara," I say. "Thanks so much." She gives me that motherly look (you know the one . . . the one you get from mothers even when they're not *your* mother) and into the armpit I go again.

"You're welcome, darling."

A parent in a waiting car honks at us to hurry up and I'm released again. "Yeah, yeah, don't get your knickers in a knot," Fara mumbles under her breath as we all pile into The Beast and disappear in a very dramatic cloud of purple smoke.

When we get to the hospital, Toby and I go in to see Olivia. She's sleeping again, but Dad says she's doing better. I brush her fringe back off her face and tuck the little stuffed hippo we bought her under her arm.

"See you soon, Liv," I whisper to her. "We've got some work to do." I put my MP3 player and a little speaker on the table next to her and flick through my playlist until I find "Diamonds on the Soles of Her Shoes".

While Dad's getting coffee and Paul Simon is singing softly to Olivia, Toby and I slip out and head to the gift shop. We stand there as I look around the mass of flowers, toys and balloons.

"Grab anything that doesn't have glitter," I instruct Toby. "You know how I feel about glitter." We whip around the small shop grabbing teddies and chocolates and balloons that say "Get Well Soon".

"Um, can I help you kids?"

I spin round, arms crammed with gifts, to find myself face to face with a rather unimpressed-looking shop assistant peering down at me through

115

her thin rectangle glasses.

"We're just picking up some things," I say, thinking that'll be the end of the conversation.

"Yes, well, this is a gift shop, and we ask that if you can't pay for it, you don't touch it."

What I can only assume is supposed to be a smile forces its way through the crusty crevices surrounding the woman's mouth. I don't like her. I know they say don't judge a book by its cover . . . but I'm judging. Before I say whatever smart thing is about to come out of my mouth, Toby steps between us. Piling his load on top of mine so that I can't even see over the gifts, he smiles sweetly at the lady.

"It's OK," he says confidently. "We've got the money to pay for it." Toby pulls a double handful of notes out of his bag and thrusts them in her face. And then something weird happens. She sort of backs away from it like it's a handful of spiders and puts her hands in the air, like she wants nothing to do with it.

"Where did you kids get that kind of money?" she says accusingly, her eyes narrowing. Toby stalls. I suddenly realise that two ten-year-olds with five grand in cash is not normal. Not normal at all. The shop lady's face confirms this. As her eyes narrow on Toby, I step in.

"Oh, it's not OUR money," I say, searching my brain for a reason we'd have the money. "We were given it. It's our job to go and choose all the presents for the kids."

I watch her eyes un-narrow a bit. "Given it? From whom?" she asks.

"From, um, a donation."

I watch her relax and her eyes widen. "Oh, are you charity shoppers?"

I smile at her. "Obviously," I say. I mean, it *is* obvious. It's not correct, but it's obvious.

"Oh, OK," she says, gathering the gifts from us. "Such good kids. We don't get many kids volunteering these days. You know, with all the technology and things, kids just don't seem very into giving. But you two . . . that's wonderful. Let me help you."

"Wow, that turned around quickly," Toby whispers to me.

"Yeah. Let's not go flashing around our wads

of cash from now on, huh, Tobes?" I suggest. "I guess kids shouldn't really be carrying around thousands of dollars, right?" Toby nods and stuffs the money back into his bag.

The cranky shop lady rings up our stuff and takes our money. She pats me on the head. "Now, you be careful with that change and make sure you get it back safe," she says. I try not to laugh at the hundred or so dollars in my hand when I think about the ten thousand in Toby's backpack.

Toby notes down the money we spent into his ledger and attaches the receipt. We grab our stuff and head back to the children's ward.

And the fun begins.

The children's ward is full of kids hooked up to machines, kids covered in bandages, kids with crutches and wheelchairs and – well, there are some kids that I'm not even sure why they're in hospital. But they're all loving the toys and balloons and mountains of stuffed animals. Bears are tossed from bed to bed and helium balloons bob around the ceiling.

I'm standing next to the bed of a boy who has a breathing tank. I tie a helium fish balloon to the tank as I tell him a version of a story I've told Olivia before.

"So the scuba diver takes his tank and dives down and down, deep below the water where he enters a whole new world where fish rule. And on the weekends they take their human-ing rods and go human-ing for the biggest human they can catch. Then they lie to their fishy friends about how big that human really was." As the fish bounces around over our heads, I turn to him. "Now, this guy here is the king of fish world and he's gonna keep an eye on you for a while, ok?"

The boy nods and tugs on the string to make the fish bounce around. He giggles softly and his mum smiles at him. "Thank you," she says. "You guys were great today. Where are you from?"

"Oh, just down in Watterson," I say.

She laughs. "No, I mean, what charity or company are you from?"

"Oh, um . . ."

"Treasure Chest Treats," Toby says as he walks up beside me. "See, I can think on my feet too," he says under his breath.

"Well, you guys have been amazing," says the mum. "It's such a great idea to have kids come in. I mean, the normal volunteers are really nice and everything, but it's just not the same. I hope you come back."

I nod. "We will." And I mean it.

We finish our "rounds" and head out to wait for Fara.

Toby punches me in the arm. "You did good, Tess."

"*We* did good, Toby." Then I punch him in the arm twice as hard. "And don't punch me!"

Toby rubs his arm as Fara pulls up in The Beast.

TIP 17

DON'T PUNCH PEOPLE.
Even if you're trying to be cool. If they punch harder, you lose.

14

Not So Kooky

So you know how that last bit ended with Toby and me standing side by side, resolute that we were going to do great things, gazing out into a bright future, something like "We are the Champions" playing as the scene faded to black? Yeah, well, here's what we learnt over the next few days.

TIP 18

IT'S NOT THAT EASY TO SPEND A MILLION DOLLARS WHEN YOU'RE TEN. (EVEN WHEN YOU WANT TO DO GOOD WITH IT.)

Adults get suspicious when two ten-year-olds are running around with wad-loads of cash. They don't want to take the money. They want to know where it came from. They draw A LOT of attention to you (which you really don't want) and they ask WAY too many questions. The limit that you can flash at an adult without all of the above kicking off is about fifty dollars. And there are a LOT of fifty-dollar notes in a million dollars.

"Aaaarrrggghh! It's just so frustrating," I say, kicking an empty soft drink can as we walk through Brennan Park.

"I know, Tess, but I don't know what we can do," says Toby as he bends down to pick up the can and toss it in a nearby recycling bin.

"Hey, I was kicking that!"

Toby rolls his eyes at me. I hate it when he does that. It's my thing. "How are we supposed to do all the stuff on our list if every time we try to spend any money, a grown-up gets in the way?" Toby shrugs, which is about as helpful as the eye rolling.

We've had a frustrating week. After deciding all the good things we wanted to do with our money, we set about putting our plans into action, but were stopped at every turn by a suspicious or concerned adult. Suspicious or concerned adults are THE WORST! So we've achieved pretty much nothing, and Toby's backpack is almost as full of cash as it was at the beginning of the week.

"This isn't how it goes in the movies," I say, looking for something else to kick. "By now we should be driving around in Ferraris and have fixed world hunger."

"You can't even drive, Tess, and I'm pretty sure it's going to take more than a million dollars to fix world hunger. It affects over 815 million people."

"Great, thanks, Toby. So not only can I not spend the money, but even if I could, it wouldn't help. You're such a great best friend to have around. Really know how to make me feel better." I glare at Toby and consider kicking him.

On top of everything, Olivia's still not out of hospital. Dad promises it'll be soon, but it's not soon enough. I hate going to visit her there. I hate the colour of the walls. I hate how that big bed makes her look so small. And I hate how guilty I feel every time I visit, knowing it's my fault she's there. I want her home. Where I can keep her safe.

"If you can't find what you want, perhaps what you want is not what you need."

A scratchy voice and an out-of-tune guitar pierce my thoughts. I was so annoyed that I forgot to bypass Kooky Kathy's bench. She's perched up on top of the seat like a chicken, strumming away on her guitar. "Ideas are like a grown-up tree, but first you gotta plant the seed."

Toby smiles and heads towards her. I don't argue. Maybe a little Kooky Kathy tune will distract me.

"Elvis!" she shouts as we approach.

"Hey, Kathy," Toby says as he sits and pulls up a bit of grass in front of her bench.

"Ooohhh and you brought Lennon." She winks at me. I have no idea what she's talking about, but later I Googled it and it turns out Lennon was the "serious one" of The Beatles. I think she was making fun of me.

Kathy's clothes are hanging all over the branches of the tree next to her bench, creating a sort of washing line tent. Next to her, she has a shopping trolley full of stuff she's collected, or maybe stuff Mr Piddles has collected. Either way it all looks like junk to me. Feeling like a hippie (and not liking it), I sit down on the ground next to Toby.

"What's with the clothes?" I ask.

"Oh, big rains last night," says Kathy. "All my stuff got soaked. It's the downside of living in the park, I guess. Upside is I have a really big garden." She laughs at her own joke and picks out a soft tune on her guitar. We all just sit there in the sun for a moment, and I have to say, while making it very clear I'm no hippie, it's kind of relaxing. I look at Kathy. I haven't noticed before, but under that mass of greying hair with the purple streak, she has quite nice eyes. They're a funny colour – kind of green/grey – and they sort of sparkle. It's a sparkle that I always thought was a little crazy, but today it looks more exciting and daring. I guess it's a fine line sometimes.

"Hey, Kathy . . ."

"Yes, Lennon."

I let that slide. "Why do you live in the park?" I ask. I try to put the next bit gently. "Don't you have family or someone you could live with?"

"I did, a while back," she says as she moves from plucking to strumming a tune. "Now Mr Piddles is my family." That should be sad, but she doesn't seem so sad about it. Her eyes sort of dance when she mentions that weird rodent. Suddenly I'm very aware that I don't know where he is. And that creeps me out a little.

I look at the clothes hanging on the tree around Kathy. It doesn't seem fair – she may be weird and her family might be a ferret, but she still deserves somewhere to live.

"Wait!" I jump to my feet, startling Toby. But everything startles Toby. "I've got it." I grab Toby's bag and fish out handfuls of cash, thrusting them towards Kathy.

"Here! Take it! You could get a nice hotel . . . with a shower. And buy some new clothes and even a new guitar. One that's in tune, maybe. And get singing lessons . . ." I stop. I think that might have been rude, but I'm sure she gets the idea. "Then you wouldn't have to live in the park any more. You could have a real home."

Kathy laughs at me. I find this annoying considering I just offered to rescue her from her kooky life.

"Oh, Lennon," she says, shaking her head. "I don't want to leave the park, and I definitely don't want to live in some stuffy hotel room. Who would feed the possums at night? And what about Mr Piddles? You think they would let him in some fancy-shmancy hotel? Nope, I'm good, thanks. Money's not my thing."

"Money's not your thing?" I shout. "What does that even mean? How can money not be your thing? It's everybody's thing. You can't do anything without it."

She laughs at me again (which is seriously starting to annoy me) and breaks into a high-pitched rendition of "Can't Buy Me Love".

"Surely you know this one, Lennon."

I've had enough. I storm off as Toby gives chase. He grabs my arm and I spin round. "What, Toby?"

"Not everyone wants the same things, Tess. And that doesn't make them wrong. It just makes them different."

"But how can she want to live in the park? It doesn't make sense."

"To you, maybe. But she's not the same as you."

"It's just so frustrating that we can't help anyone," I say, throwing my bag to the ground.

"No, we just can't help them *your* way." Toby picks my bag up and hands it back to me.

"But look at all her stuff." I point to the washing line tree. "She can't love being drenched every time it rains, no matter how much of a hippie she is."

"True, but that doesn't mean she wants to live in a hotel. Maybe she just needs some shelter. Not everything is an easy fix."

I stop. "Sometimes you have to be creative." I feel an idea forming. It's my favourite feeling. "Toby, tell every kid you can to meet us here in the park at nine am tomorrow. There's twenty dollars in it for every kid that shows up."

"ok, but . . ."

"I'll fill you in tonight," I call over my shoulder as I run off. "Nine am tomorrow. As many kids as you can."

"We're supposed to walk home together!" I hear him shout as I run across the park.

I know that's the rule. But sometimes even rules have to be flexible.

TIP 19

_____

YOU SHOULD FOLLOW RULES BECAUSE YOU BELIEVE THEY ARE RIGHT. NOT JUST BECAUSE THEY ARE SO.

Most rules are there for a reason and make sense. But you also need to remember to follow rules because you think they're right, not just because someone tells you to. Did you know there used to be a rule that women couldn't vote? Or that not everybody could marry the person they love? There was even a law that made it illegal to be in possession of more than fifty kilograms of potatoes. So, you know, rules change, but doing what you believe is right doesn't.

_____

15

Home is Where the Ferret is

So Toby did good, as Toby usually does, and now I'm standing in Brennan Park with about fifty kids waiting for instructions. Toby starts handing out the money. Every kid gets fifty dollars, plus a twenty for them to keep. I can almost see the dollar signs lighting up in their eyes. *Yeah right, Toby. As if money isn't everyone's thing.*

"All right, guys, here's what you need to do," I announce to the excited crowd. "Everyone pocket the twenty. That's for you, for helping us out on your Saturday morning. I need everyone to take the fifty, go to Watto Mall and buy fifty dollars worth of Lego. Spread out. Go to different stores.

If you come back and have time to do a second trip, you'll get another twenty. But only buy one lot of Lego at a time, and try not to be directly after another kid. We don't want to attract too much attention. Got it?"

Everyone nods and heads off. That's the best thing about us kids. We don't ask a lot of questions.

Toby and I watch them run off. "Do you reckon any of them will just take the fifty and disappear?"

Toby shakes his head. "Nah, I don't."

I feel like he's being very optimistic. But that's Toby.

$

Turns out Toby was right. Not only did every kid come back, but most did a second trip and didn't even want another twenty. By late morning, Watto Mall was completely out of Lego and there was a mountain of toyshop bags at Brennan Park.

"What now?" asks one of the kids.

I look at Toby. "Well, that's it really. We just couldn't go and spend all that money at once, 'cos adults keep getting suspicious. So, you know, thanks?"

"But what are you gonna do with all the Lego?" asks another kid.

"Toby and I are going to build a shelter for a lady who lives here in the park."

"Kooky Kathy? Awesome! She's a right laugh."

"Yeah. Can we help?"

"I'm really good at Lego."

"And we could build a little house for Mr Piddles too."

Before Toby and I can even answer, they're on the job – tearing open boxes, sorting Lego into piles of different sizes and colours and planning a layout and design. They scurry around like ants, working together as the base of a small, cubby-sized shelter begins to form. It's pretty amazing to watch. I mean, we're talking about kids who can barely organise a footy game at break, and yet here they are, working together to build a Lego house.

"Is that Dane?" I follow Toby's pointed finger. Standing on the far side of the park area is my brother, directing a bunch of Year Threes to make the base out of eight-by-two pieces. Then he sections off another group of kids, hands them a mixed bucket, shows them some kind of plan and they're off to work.

"Do you think he'll ask where the money came from?" I say.

"Maybe, but you know it's going to be hard to keep it a secret from everyone."

Dane runs after Butthead, who's chasing himself around a tree. I shake my head. "Nah, not from Dane. Don't worry about it. He probably just heard there was a Lego party and couldn't resist. If he asks anything just play dumb, like he does."

At this point, I have to admit I step back and let everyone do their thing. I'm not being lazy – ideas are my thing, and I'm the first to admit that there are people who are better than me at other things. Toby's a great organiser. Apparently, Tako from 5B is a future architect because he's completely redesigning the roof I had in mind, and Dane has even worked out a way to make a sliding door. I do what I do best – assure passers-by that yes, it's a school installation art project, and of course the Council knows about it, and I've got the permit here somewhere (I pat my pockets and look around, eventually getting distracted by a very important construction consultation).

And in between, I'm watching this shelter grow before my eyes. Cue Lego building montage to the tune of "Sweet Dreams" by The Eurythmics. I walk between the workers, rubbing my chin and pointing out helpful observations. See, I know what it takes to be a good manager.

TIP 20

"A MANAGER IS NOT A PERSON WHO CAN DO THE WORK BETTER THAN HIS MEN. HE IS A PERSON WHO CAN GET HIS MEN TO DO THE WORK BETTER THAN HIM."

So I stole this tip directly from Frederick W. Smith, the CEO of FedEx. Try and ignore all the "men" and "he" bits (sometimes even really smart people can be a little sexist) – it's actually a pretty good tip. Know what you're good at and do it, then help other people do what they do best.

By late afternoon, there stands a Lego house. OK, house might be the wrong word. Shelter? Look, I'm not talking three bedrooms with a garage and pool-room, but it'll keep the rain off Kathy. It's about the size of a playhouse with a pyramid-shaped roof, an opening at the front that she'll have to duck to get into and a couple of simple windows. It even has a mini-house for that little rodent of hers. I have to say, it's pretty cool.

Toby gets some fish and chips for everyone and passes them round. Soon we're all munching away.

"Cool, huh?" he says.

I nod. "Do you think anyone will have a problem with it being here?"

"Two steps ahead of you, Tess," Toby says and ducks off, coming back with a poster rolled under his arm. "I threw this together at my mums' shop while I was waiting for the fish and chips. It's not my best work, but hopefully it'll buy us a bit of time."

He unrolls the poster and holds it up.

WATTERSON CREATIVE ART DISPLAY

MODERN ART INSTALLATION BY YEAR FIVE
OF WATTERSON PRIMARY

SPONSORED BY COPY CATS PRINT SHOP

PLEASE NO CLIMBING ON THE ARTWORK

I raise my eyebrows. "Sponsored by Copy Cats, huh?"

"Throwing in a bit of free advertising for the print shop doesn't hurt. Plus, I think it adds to the legitimacy."

I can't help but laugh as I snatch the poster from him. "I'm starting to think I'm rubbing off on you, Toby."

"Never!" he says, and we stick the poster up in front of the Lego house.

Leaving everyone else to their fish and chips, I go get Kathy.

"So what do you reckon?" I ask her, gesturing dramatically towards the multi-coloured structure. A huge smile spreads across Kathy's face.

"I love it. It's so colourful. What's it for?"

"It's for you, Kathy. Well, the big one is. The little one is for Mr Piddles." I try to stop my nose from screwing up when I say his name.

Kathy bites her lip. "For us?"

"Yeah. You know, so you have somewhere to keep your stuff and you don't get wet when it rains. A home, but without leaving the park." Kathy's eyes start to get a bit wet. Oh no, I really hope she doesn't cry. I get super-awkward when people cry. Especially adults. "It's no big deal," I say, shrugging my shoulders to prove it.

"Yes, it is," says Kathy. She grabs Mr Piddles and heads inside to take a look.

"It's not much but you could put your bed . . . mat . . . thing over there. And some of your stuff there."

Mr Piddles jumps out of Kathy's hands and runs straight into his little house.

"He likes it!" I shout. I'm not sure why I'm seeking approval from a ferret, but it does feel good.

"We don't like it, we love it," says Kathy. "Thank you, Lennon. So much. If there's anything I can ever do to repay you, just ask."

Her eyes are getting wet again.

"Nope, that's fine. Just enjoy." Without another word I duck outside to where all the kids are sitting around eating. "Hey, thanks, everyone. You did awesome!"

A cheer erupts from the kids and Kooky Kathy comes out with her guitar. She breaks into "Imagine" by John Lennon. Not my favourite song, and Kathy's out of tune voice doesn't help, but I don't say anything. Instead, I sit down with Toby and grab some of his chips. We enjoy our greasy snack under the sun, the words of "Imagine" floating around and a general feeling of achievement hovering over us.

"Bit of a feel-good moment, huh?" Toby says with a grin.

I stuff a chip in my mouth.

It does feel kind of good, but I'll never admit that to Toby.

Kathy finishes the song and shifts into "Diamonds on the Soles of Her Shoes" – Olivia's favourite. Toby reads my mind. He knows how much she loves this song.

"I wish she was here too," he says.

"No," I answer. "Liv gets out of hospital today and she's having nothing to do with our list, ok, Toby?"

"Not even the good stuff?"

I shake my head. "None of it. I don't want her involved."

"But she'd love what we're doing," says Toby softly.

"I don't care. Look what happened last time." I stare at Toby hard, making sure he gets my point. "Nothing to do with it. Got me?"

Toby just nods and returns to his piece of fish.

I walk home with Dane and Butthead. I hate walking with Butthead because he likes to walk between your feet instead of next to you like a normal dog.

"That was pretty cool," says Dane. "Building that thing for Kathy."

I'm worried this is going to lead to questions. "Yeah, just a school project Toby and I are working on." Dane tosses a stick to try to get Butthead out from under our feet. I notice the black FitBit on his wrist and grab the opportunity to change the subject.

"Where'd you get the FitBit?" I ask casually.

"Oh, Kathy gave it to me," he says, turning the black band on his wrist. "Mr Piddles found it. It's so cool, she taught him how to fetch stuff that looks like certain things. She's gonna show me how, and I'm gonna teach Butthead to fetch me a whole bunch of lost FitBits. Then I could start a second-hand FitBit store."

I bite my tongue to stop myself from saying what I think of this idea. I mean, Butthead just got distracted trying to fetch a stick and is now barking angrily at a pinecone.

"Do you really think you can teach him to do that?" I ask.

"Sure I can. You underestimate him, Tess. He's as smart as Mr Piddles." Butthead forgives the pinecone, grabs the stick and trots back over to Dane, dropping it at his feet. "See?" Dane says.

I bite down hard on my tongue and nod.

That night, I sit at my desk watching the spinning wheel of death on my hand-me-down laptop. It's so frustrating. I have a million dollars sitting under my bed and I can't even buy myself a new computer. I was shopping around online checking out the latest laptops – which I had convinced myself would help me help the world, you know, more efficiently – but you can't buy anything online without a credit card. I look at everything on our list. I pretty much can't do *any* of it without a credit card. When did we stop using good old cash? I roll my eyes at myself. Great, now I sound like Dad. He saw someone pay for something with their watch the other day and flipped out. I was totally embarrassed by his technological bafflement but now I sympathise just a little. Maybe things were easier back in Dad's "good old days". In a true sign of desperation, I get up and head to Sash's room.

I sneak past Olivia's door. She's home from hospital, but has pretty much been sleeping since I got back from the park.

I stop outside Sash's room and knock. No answer. I push the door open. She's at her desk editing her latest video.

"Excuse me!" Sash says, pulling her earphones out. "Try knocking."

"I did," I sigh. "You didn't hear me. You were plugged."

"Whatever. What do you want?"

"How did you buy that second-hand speaker on eBay last month? Didn't you need a credit card?"

"Yeah, of course I did."

OK, this sounds good. "You have a credit card?"

Sash laughs at me. Not so good. She looks at me like I'm an idiot, which is ironic really. "I'm sixteen, Tess. You think Mum and Dad would let me have a credit card? Only adults can get credit cards. Mum paid for it with hers and I paid her back with my pocket money."

"Oh," I say and then, just before Sash plugs back in, "Do you know how you get a credit card?"

"Nah, but Mum said I can get a debit card if I can get my savings up to five hundred."

"What's a debit card?" I ask.

Sash sighs dramatically. "I thought you Googled everything these days?"

I just cross my arms and glare at her. She rolls her eyes at me. It *is* annoying.

"It's like a credit card, but you can only spend the money that you have in your account. So you can shop online and stuff, but you can't actually get credit. You know, so you're just spending your own money. Not the bank's."

"How do I get one?" I ask.

"*You* don't get one. You have to be like sixteen. Then you open an account, go into a bank with your ID and boom! Debit card." Sash plugs back in. "Leave now," she says as she waves her hand, dismissing me.

I close the door.

I know what to do.

I sneak downstairs. Mum and Dad are watching TV. Mum's bag sits on the kitchen table. I feel bad, but what I'm about to do is just borrowing. I'll put it back. I slide her driving licence out from behind a photo of us kids. She reckons she prefers to look at *our* faces in that little plastic window than her own, but I know she just hates her licence picture. I straighten up the family photo so you can't tell anything's missing from behind. It's a pretty cute photo. It was taken just after Jake was born and I think it might be the last photo we all had together.

I snap the wallet shut, stuff it back into Mum's bag and head to the filing cabinet in the study. It's easy to find what I need here – it was me who organised the filing system. I run my fingers over Mum's birth certificate. It feels old and precious. That little voice is trying to make itself heard but I silence it. It's just borrowing. I'll bring it back. I make a promise to myself to take the best care of it as I slip the certificate under my T-shirt and head back upstairs to my room. Within fifteen minutes, the online application for a brand new debit account is complete, and my plan has been put into action. Toby is *not* going to like this one. But what's new?

16

Rent-a-Mum

Toby waits for me at Brennan Park like I told him to. I gloss over my plan and, as expected, he's not happy.

"There's a line, Tess, and I think this is crossing it."

"It's not like we're spending anyone else's money – we can only spend the money we put into the account. It's no different to what we've been doing, except that we'll be able to do it online." I can feel myself getting frustrated. We don't have time for this.

"It is different, Tess. It's called fraud and I'm pretty sure it's illegal."

"It's not fraud! Stop being so dramatic."

I Googled fraud later, and Toby's pretty much right. But like I said at the beginning, I made loads of mistakes. This is one of them.

"Big picture, Toby," I say as I drag him off. "You gotta think big picture."

Kooky Kathy doesn't take too much convincing. She's so grateful for her new home that I'm pretty sure she'd do anything to help us.

Our first stop is Toby's house. Both his mums are at the print shop, so it's easy to sneak Kathy in for a quick shower.

"Make sure you wash your hair!" I call through the closed bathroom door, but the only response I get is the sound of Kathy singing in the shower. When she comes out she swears she used the shampoo, but her hair looks as wild as usual to me. She throws on one of Fara's old tracksuits and we head into Watterson.

The three of us sit in Stylize Beauty Studio as the hairdresser plucks at Kathy's matted hair like a two-year-old picking peas out of their dinner. His nose screws up and he leans away from Kathy as he asks, "And what are we doing today?"

Before Kathy has a chance to answer, I shove a photo of Mum towards him.

"Make her look like that?" I say. I can tell by his face that apparently it's a big ask. It's true Kathy currently has greyish-brown hair with a purple streak that could be anywhere between curly and a bird's nest. The photo of Mum shows straight blond hair. I can see he's not sure. "Or as close as you can get," I say.

The hairdresser squeezes his hands into rubber gloves.

"This will take a while," he says, rolling his eyes. OK, I can *really* see why that annoys people now.

"No problem, we have stuff to do anyway. We'll come back."

"OK, but this is all going to cost a bit. Who's paying?" He casts a doubtful eye towards Kathy, who's amusing herself with a gossip magazine.

"Oh yeah. We are, it's fine. Toby?"

Toby grabs a handful of cash from his bag and hands it to the hairdresser.

A look I'm now very familiar with passes across his face. It's the look that says, "Where did you kids get that kind of money?"

"We've been saving up. It's her birthday present," I say quickly. "Dad helped pay." I watch the look disappear.

"OK, cool. Well, see you in a couple of hours. Your mum will be a new woman."

"That's what I'm counting on," I mumble as I drag Toby out of the salon.

At this point, people might think I've crossed some sort of line. That I've gone too far. But as Hippocrates says (or said), "desperate times call for desperate measures". That means when there's no other way, do it the Tess way. Or, at least, that's how I translate it.

You would have heard people say "things aren't always black or white". I really truly believe that. Like we all know we're not supposed to lie, right? But when Toby's mums decided to try the Cuts for Charity hairdressers and Toby ended up with a big wonky shaved spot on the back of his head and he asked me, "Is it that bad?" . . . well, I said no. Now that was a total lie. He looked like he'd been in a fight with a lawn mower and lost. But telling him that would have made him feel worse. Adults do this too, so they start to sub-categorise lies. They've invented white lies, half-truths, exaggeration, omission, error, restructuring . . . they're all just lies. So when adults say you should always tell the truth, here's what I say . . .

TIP 21

WORRY LESS ABOUT WHETHER SOMETHING IS A LIE AND MORE ABOUT WHAT THAT LIE WILL DO.
I mean, you should try to tell the truth whenever you can. Of course. But it's unlikely you'll get through life telling only the entire truth. What you DO need to think about is "what are the consequences of lying". Will it hurt someone? Will it hurt you? Is it wrong? And that brings us back to **Tip 7** – listen to that little voice. It will help you here too.

So yes, my actions so far might not put me in the running for the Nobel Peace Prize (seriously, that thing is REALLY hard to win), but I had a plan and I was going to see it through. I have to get some credit for that, right?

Toby and I go to the mall to pick up some new clothes for Kathy. We buy one piece from each shop, stick with the "Mum's birthday" story, and pay for it all in cash. I buy her a purse and stick some money in it. We head to the food court and grab a rewards card from every place that has them to fill up the cards section of the purse. I buy a photo frame and some scissors from the discount store, then I pull out the stock photo of the family from the frame and cut out the kids, shoving it into the little clear plastic bit of the purse. And, finally, I slide Mum's driving licence into the front slit. Mum's photo stares back at me and I feel totally guilty. Is it possible that even though that picture was taken three years ago I can see disapproval in her eyes?

"You sure about this, Tess?" Toby asks. Seriously, can that kid read my mind?

"Totally sure." I snap the purse shut. *Big picture, Tess. You gotta think of the big picture.*

By the time we get back to the salon, it's almost eleven. We have to get a move on. I burst in past the pretty mums and dads waiting to get their hair and nails done and straight to the hairdresser. He's now working on the grey hair of some lady who smells way too strongly of lavender perfume.

"Hey there. Hi," I say, trying to pull his attention away from the creamed scalp he's focused on. "Sorry, we have to go. Where is she?"

"Um, right there," he says, pointing to the waiting area.

One of the pretty mums waves at us. Toby and I stop and stare.

"Is that . . . ?" Toby mumbles.

The lady in front of us can't be Kathy. Her skin is glowing, her nails are shiny, her hair is straight and blond and . . . clean.

"It can't be . . ." I say as the lady continues to grin back at me. She picks up her guitar and starts singing "I Feel Good". The entire salon looks at her in disapproval.

"Yup, that's her," I say, and we get out of there before they throw us out.

"You look great, Kathy!" Toby says. "How do you feel?"

"I feel the same, little Elvis. Clothes don't maketh the woman!"

"Well, they better maketh the mum," I say, turning on them. "OK, you both know the plan?"

"Are you sure you're OK with this, Kathy?" Toby asks. My teeth clench. We've been through this a million times.

"Like I said, kids, it's your plan. I'm just here to help. If you're good with it, then who am I to tell you what to do." Kathy lifts up her guitar. "We all have to walk our own path in life."

Worried she's about to sing again, I take the guitar and pass it to Toby.

"We're good with it," I answer for both of us. "Wait here for us, Toby. You ready, Kathy?"

"Who's Kathy? I think you mean Jennifer Heckleston of 14 Wyndeman Close, Watterson. You know, I always dreamed of being a performer on stage. Perhaps this is my break-out role."

"Yeah, maybe," I say, leading her towards the bank. "Let's go, Julia Roberts!"

Remember how I said adults can underestimate kids? Well, sometimes kids can underestimate adults. As we wait at the bank for our number to be called, my hands start to sweat a little. The piece of paper I'm holding with the big black B46 on it is going soggy. Kathy, however, looks as cool as a cucumber. That's a Dad saying. I don't understand why a cucumber would be any cooler than the other vegetables in the fridge. Finally, our number dings and Kathy walks over to the counter.

It takes all my self-control not to speak for her. I have to play the kid in this charade, and I have to trust that my rehearsals with Kathy will pay off.

Kathy rests her new purse on the counter and suddenly looks remarkably un-kooky. She slides the printed application I gave her towards the bank lady.

"Good afternoon. My name is Jennifer Heckleston. I'm here to open an account that I applied for online."

The bank lady smiles a cheesy sort of smile at her. We must have done a good job at the salon, because normally Kathy gets a very different kind of look.

"Absolutely, Ms Heckleston. Can I please see your ID?"

Kathy whips Mum's driving licence out of her purse. She pulls out Mum's birth certificate, unfolds it and slides the two documents towards the bank lady. Bank-lady taps at her keyboard, then holds the licence photo up in front of Kathy, who attempts to mimic the face my mum is pulling in the photo. I hold my breath. I worry that it's too much, but bank-lady seems satisfied.

"Great," she says, "I can see here that your account has been approved. So I'll just make a copy of your ID, and we'll get you sorted."

I release my breath. I've done it. The next few minutes of signing papers and entering codes goes by in a blur. Kathy's on fire, chatting casually and answering all the lady's questions without hesitation. I have to admit, I'm kind of impressed.

"OK, Jennifer. Now that's sorted, I'll get your debit card. You have a choice of blue, black or pink."

"Oh, pink please!" Kathy says.

"I like the pink ones too," bank-lady giggles. What? Now they're besties?

Bank-lady disappears to get the card and I slide nine thousand dollars into Kathy's lap.

"Woah," says Kathy. "You don't think this much cash is a bit suspect?"

"I Googled it," I say under my breath. "Anything under ten thousand doesn't raise attention. This is nine. Just stick to the story."

"Oh no, I have a way better one," says Kathy, and before I can object, bank-lady returns with her cheesy smile.

"Here you go," she says, wiggling the card in front of Kathy like it's dancing. "Now, are we going to make a deposit today?"

"Oh, yes please," says Kathy as she plonks the nine thousand cash in front of bank-lady.

"Wow," the bank-lady says, her eyes lighting up just a little. "How much do we have here?"

"Only nine thousand," Kathy says, rolling her eyes. I hope she didn't get that from me. "I just sold my Fender signed by The Eagles. I wanted twelve for it, but I was talked down."

I have no idea what Kathy's talking about and I'm not sure bank-lady does either, but she seems happy and deposits the money. Before I know it, we're walking out of the bank, proud owners of a brand new debit card.

"Show it to me," Toby says. Kathy passes him the card. His eyes widen. "Ooohhh, I like the colour."

"Right?" says Kathy. I snatch the card.

"OK, we have work to do," I say, not wanting to waste any more time. "You each have your bundles and here's the sort code and account number. Remember, deposit only one bundle per branch. Use the ATM deposits. We have to fly under the radar. We meet back at Brennan Park at two o'clock. Got it?"

They nod and we all head our separate ways. I'm feeling good. We have a plan and things are starting to work out. I smile to myself as I run my finger over the raised numbers of the debit card. Today is a good day. I've got this.

$

At two o'clock I head back to Brennan Park to meet Toby and Kathy. It's crowded – some big event is happening on the far side. I resist the urge to go check it out, and hunt for the others. I finally spot them and head over to tally our work. We've managed to deposit a massive $90,000.

"What now?" asks Toby.

"What now?" I say. "Toby, now we can do anything. We can buy anything. The sky's the limit!"

"Well, technically ninety thousand dollars is the limit," says Kathy and laughs at her own joke. "So how do you want to celebrate?"

"What do you reckon, Toby?" I say. "Ice cream? Pizza? New iPhones?"

Toby shakes his head. "I have the perfect idea."

He drags us towards the crowd of people gathered at the far end of the park. There's a big tent set up and balloons and umbrellas and best of all . . . PUPPIES!

"It's a fundraiser for the Guide Dogs," Toby says. "This HAS to be the first thing we do. Pleeeeeease!"

Now, normally I'm pretty careful about how I spend my money, but you should have seen these puppies! Even I couldn't resist the urge to throw money at them. They were fluffy and golden and tripping all over each other. Then, in another part of the park, the grown-up dogs that were all well behaved and clever were showing how they helped people get around. I don't know if it was the high of the debit card in my hand or the power of the puppies, but I was sold!

TIP 22

NO ONE CAN RESIST PUPPIES.
If you ever want to get someone over the line on a deal – bring a puppy. Seriously. No one can say no to a puppy.

I pass the card to Kathy.

"How much are we donating?" she asks.

I look at Toby and his big Chihuahua eyes. I look at the puppies falling over their own feet. And before I can stop the words coming out of my mouth . . .

"A thousand."

"Woah," says Toby. "Cool."

Kathy smiles at me. "Someone's getting soft in their old age."

"Maybe," I say, and we walk over to the tent to donate our money.

Now, here's something I didn't know about giving money to charity. I mean, it's not something I normally do. But you know . . . the puppies!

Apparently at these things people donate a couple of dollars, or maybe a hundred if they REALLY like the puppies. It turns out a thousand is kind of a big deal. So next thing, we're being swamped by people shaking our hands and taking photos. A guy with a big camera lines us up in front of the Guide Dog banner and passes me a puppy, and Kathy's shaking hands with some man who's important in the world of puppies. Announcements are being made about donation records being broken, and cheers are being shouted, and I decide it's time for us to leave before Toby buys one of the dogs.

"Wow, that was cool. But intense," says Toby as we sneak away from the crowd.

"Yeah, note to self – donating a thousand dollars to charity is *not* flying under the radar."

"Yeah, but it felt good," says Kathy, grinning and holding a yellow Guide Dog balloon. "I had a great day, kids. Really. Thanks. And if you need me for anything, you know where my Lego house is." With that, Kooky Kathy skips off.

"She's right, you know," says Toby. "It was a great day."

"And it's only the beginning, Tobes. Now that we have this baby." I dance the pink card in front of Toby's face just like the bank lady did. Then I stop myself. Not cool, Tess. Not cool.

17

The Price of Money

I have to say, the next couple of weeks are a lot of fun. We can finally spend our money, and boy do we spend! Toby and I take it in turns to decide what we're going to do with it next. It turns out there are a lot of people you can help with not a lot of money. We buy a goat for a family in Afghanistan. We adopt an orangutan in Borneo. We purchase a bunch of kids' books online and send them straight to some literacy foundations for underprivileged kids. And here's the thing that really surprises me: it's way more fun than shopping for yourself. I know everyone says that doing things for others makes you feel good, but you know what? It actually does.

And it's awesome to have Olivia home. And even more awesome that she's OK. But I've been giving her a lot of space, because she must hate me for the whole lollipop thing. Mum and Dad decided to give her a bit more time off school and she's been staying in her room a lot. I don't do her poke time or insulin injections any more, Dad takes care of all that now. Mum's gone back to work. She has a new show starting, so she's working really late nights.

"Tess! Is Toby staying for dinner?" Dad shouts from downstairs.

"What is it, Mr Heckleston?" Toby shouts back. We're in the middle of looking up a charity that builds shelters for homeless people up north.

"Thursday night – panang curry night!" comes Dad's voice. "And it's Alik, Toby. Stop with the Mister already!"

Toby loves Dad's curry, so of course he stays.

We sit down for dinner and Dad fills our bowls. Olivia's reading at the table, but Dad doesn't tell her not to any more. Not since the hospital.

"So Mum's going to miss dinner a bit next

week, with the show opening and all," Dad says apologetically. I don't know why. We're all used to it.

"What's the show, Mr Alik?" asks Toby.

"Just Alik. Um, it's *Peter Pan*."

"Again?" says Sash. "Haven't they done that show like a gazillion times?"

"Yeah, remember, they did it a few years ago and the girl playing Wendy got all stuck up in the wires," says Dane.

I point at him. "And you stole the rigging and built Butthead a body harness and hooked him up to the washing line," I laugh. "What did you call it?"

"Dog-Pan!" Dane says and we all laugh. I still remember Butthead flying around like Superman on the washing line, yapping at the clothes and running his legs in the air to go faster. "He was a natural," Dane says. "He still barks at the washing line, wanting to get back up for another go."

"Do you guys miss going to the theatre?" Dad asks. "I mean, you used to spend a lot of time there after school, waiting for Mum to finish work."

"Nah," we all say in unison.

But I'm not sure it's entirely true. I mean, we did used to have a lot of fun there. We knew that place like our own home. Dane spent hours up in the trusses playing with the rigging and the hoists, working out how they operated. Sash practically lived in the AV booth, toying with the lights and projectors and video screens. I'd be at the ticket counter, counting money, working out the profits and devising ways to increase ticket sales. But that was ages ago. Back when we were little kids. We have better things to do now.

"Because we could go there sometimes and visit Mum if you wanted to," Dad offers.

Olivia lifts her head up from the book. "That could be cool," she says. "If we all went together."

"Nah, I've gotta work on Butthead's trailer," says Dane.

"Yeah, Toby and I have stuff to do too," I say.

"And I just don't want to," says Sash as she picks up her half-eaten dinner and dumps it in the bin. "I'm going back to my room."

Olivia sighs and buries her head back in her book. I feel a bit bad, but with her being sick and all it's probably better that she stays in bed instead of going to that dusty old theatre.

That night there's a soft tap at my door.

"Yeah?"

Olivia comes in and perches herself on the side of my bed. I'm working my way through the list on my laptop, so I just let her sit there for a while. After a few dramatic sighs from her, I bite.

"What do you want, Liv?"

"Can I help you and Toby with your list?"

I snap my laptop shut and spin round. "What do you know about our list?"

Olivia cowers a little and shuffles back on my bed. "Nothing really. Except that you have one, and that you're excited about it, and that it's all you've been talking about for the last few weeks. It seems like a lot of work. Maybe I could help?"

"Have you been spying on us?"

"No!" Olivia says. "I live here too, you know. You guys think you're so secretive and clever, but I know stuff as well."

"What do you know?" I have to be careful here. There's no way she could know about the money, but if she knows too much about the list . . . I can't have her getting involved.

"Just that I could help," she says quietly. "With whatever you're doing. I could, Tess."

Good. She doesn't know anything. She just wants to be part of whatever is going on. I have to keep her out of it, for her own good. I don't like what I'm about to do but . . .

"You can't help, Olivia. You're just a little kid. And you're supposed to be getting better. Go back to bed."

She stands up, her fists clenched by her side.

"I'm not little! And I'm not ill! You think just 'cos you're three years older than me that you know everything? Well, you don't."

With that, she storms out of my room and slams the door. There's a niggly feeling of guilt churning in my stomach, but I don't have time to worry about it now. I need to keep her out of things, and having her angry with me is probably the best way. I hate hurting Liv's feelings, but it's better than her actually getting hurt again. Plus, I have other important things to worry about. I have a list to get through!

$

The next day is full of red flags. Red flags are things that happen that tell you something bad is coming. I Googled it, and it turns out that red flags date way back to 1777, when they were used as a flood warning. Remember how I said to pay attention to that little inside voice? Well, pay attention to red flags too!

RED FLAG NO. 1:

I'm walking to school by myself. I know it's a no-no but Toby had to go in The Beast because he was bringing some big project to school. I'm walking through Brennan Park and I get this feeling. A creepy feeling on my skin. Like a spider is crawling across the back of my neck. I spin round. There's no one in the park except me, but I don't feel alone. In movies people always say they "feel like they're being watched" but it never really made sense to me. How can you *feel* someone watching you? Well, this is the feeling I have today. It's not a great feeling.

RED FLAG NO. 2:

I come out of class at lunchtime and find that someone has tried to open my locker. I always leave my padlock numbers on 1, 2, 3. They're now on 4, 8, 2. Kids at this school never touch each other's stuff. The spider feeling comes back even stronger, but I try to shake it off.

RED FLAG NO. 3:

At home, in my room, I look out my bedroom window. My treasure chest is open. Everything has been pulled out of it and lays scattered on the ground. The spider is doing an Irish jig on the back of my neck now. I know what this means, but I don't want to admit it. I pull the bag out from under my bed and check that all the money's still there. Safe and sound.

I ignore the little voice. I ignore the red flags. I ignore the spider.

And I head downstairs for Dad's Friday night paella instead.

Flashback Fridays is on the music channel on TV. "What I Like About You" by The Romantics is playing, so of course Dad is doing his paella dance. Olivia is already in the kitchen with Dad, but she doesn't even look at me when I come in. Seven-year-olds can really hold a grudge. She's setting the table and I start to help but she's unimpressed. As I lay down the cutlery I see the local newspaper lying in the centre of the table with the rest of the post. There, smack bang on the front page, is a photo of Kathy shaking hands with the guide dog man as she hands over our donation. Underneath is written:

GENEROUS LOCAL THEATRE MANAGER JENNIFER HECKLESTON DONATES $1000 TO GUIDE DOG FUNDRAISER.

I snatch the paper off the table and stuff it under the sofa cushion. I turn back to the kitchen. Dad's attention is fully focused on the paella, and he doesn't go through the post until after dinner, so I can safely assume he hasn't seen it. Plus, it's common knowledge that nobody ACTUALLY reads the local newspaper. It's usually full of cat rescues and baking competitions.

I grab the cutlery again and stop. Olivia's staring at me, her brow furrowed like she's trying to solve some puzzle. I shake my head and roll my eyes at her. *Just leave it alone, Liv.*

The paella is great as usual. And after dinner Dad, Dane and I settle in to watch a movie – a typical Heckleston Friday night. Sash is plugged in her room and Olivia doesn't want to join us. She must still be sulking, because it's her turn to choose the movie tonight. But since she's not here, it's my turn, which is awesome.

I head to the bookcase and flick through the DVDs. Yeah, that's right. DVDs. We must be the only family on the planet who doesn't have Apple TV or Netflix or anything from the 21st century, but Dad says until we get all the way through his DVD collection, it's a waste of money. Dad's a total movie buff and has a few hundred DVDs, so I don't see us getting Netflix any time soon, unfortunately. Good news is, Dad's got great taste in movies.

I grab *The Goonies* off the shelf. I've seen it before, but I love it. Liv does too, so I know she'll be gutted she's missing it. But that's what she gets for sulking.

TIP 23

WATCH SOME MOVIES FROM THE 80S.
I know you're probably rolling your eyes right now. So was I when Dad first forced us into watching these old movies. But they're seriously so much better. OK, they have some dodgy special effects and some pretty cheesy lines, but kids were real, actual heroes back in the 80s. They didn't need adult help or superhero intervention. If there was a problem, they went out and solved it on their own. And their parents didn't even notice they were missing. Nothing was off limits for kids in the 80s.

After the movie, I drag myself upstairs. I pause in front of Olivia's door. Her light is still on and I consider going in and apologising. But I'm too tired and she needs her rest. I'll talk to her tomorrow.

I head upstairs, crawl into bed and am asleep before I know it.

I wake in a panic. It's still dark. I can't see properly, but I can definitely make out a shape hovering over me. As my eyes adjust and I try to make sense of what's happening, I recognise the person above me and the spider feeling turns into real, full-blown fear.

"Where's my money?"

I go to scream but Scotty's hand quickly covers my mouth. His face is so close, I can smell his stale cigarette breath as he whispers, "Shhhh! Be quiet and no one gets hurt. I just want my money. Where is it?" His eyes are a terrifying mix of hate and desperation. It's hard for me to believe this is the same guy who used to toss presents to me over the fence. I try to mumble into his hand.

"I'm gonna take my hand away but if you make a sound . . ." He doesn't need to finish this sentence. The look in his eyes tells me he's ready to do anything. He slowly removes his hand and I try my best not to cry.

"It's under my bed," I whisper. "In the gym bag."

He pokes his finger in my face. "Don't move. Don't make a sound." I couldn't if I wanted to. I'm frozen with fear.

Scotty reaches under the bed and yanks out the bag. He pulls it open.

"Is this some kind of joke?" he says, anger boiling to the surface of his voice.

I pry my upper body from the bed and peer over into the bag.

It's empty.

"What? I – I swear it was, I . . ." I have no idea what to say and that doesn't happen a lot. "Honestly, it was there. It *should* be there."

I hear Mum come home. She closes the door and throws her keys on the bench. Scotty pounces, wrapping his hand round my throat.

"Listen here, you little brat. I want my money back."

"It's supposed to be here," I whisper.

"Well, it's not, is it? So you'd better find it real quick otherwise you'll pay. And so will your family. You got it?"

All I can do is nod. Mum's footsteps are coming up the stairs and, before I know it, Scotty is out of the window.

A cool breeze blows through the opening, chilling the sweat on my face. I get up and slam the window closed, locking it.

I allow myself to breathe.

My breathing gets heavier. The breaths threaten to turn into sobs. I can hear Mum in Olivia's room, checking on her. She closes Liv's door and I silently beg her to come to my room next. Her footsteps head back downstairs. I want to cry, but I won't. That Scotty jerk will NOT make me cry.

So I don't cry.

But I also don't sleep much that night.

$

"What do you mean you don't know where it is?" Toby's doing the shaking Chihuahua thing.

I rang him first thing this morning to come over. At first, it felt better having him in my room and not being alone. But now that he's shouting at me, I'm reconsidering the decision.

"Don't shout at me. It's not my fault," I shout back. "It was here one minute and then it was gone. So that's what I mean . . . I don't know where it is!"

"Well, it can't have just disappeared. And now we have some crazy killer sneaking into bedrooms at night demanding back money that you've lost!"

I roll my eyes at Toby. Whatever. He deserves it.

"First of all, we don't know that he's a crazy killer."

"Well, he went to jail for something," Toby mutters under his breath.

I ignore him. "And secondly, I didn't *lose* the money."

"Do you know where it is?"

"No."

"Then it's lost!"

Toby's really starting to get on my nerves. The heat prickles at my neck. I hate that he's the only one that can fire me up like this. I'm so angry with him I barely notice the door crack open. Olivia sticks her head in.

"Are you guys OK?" she asks.

Toby paints on a fake smile. "We're fine, Olivia. Just having a . . . discussion. Trying to work something out."

"Maybe I can help?" she says quietly.

My anger towards Toby is redirected at Olivia before I can stop it. I turn on her. "You can't help, Olivia. Just leave us alone. This isn't a little kid problem." I regret it instantly. The hurt on her face is hard to miss.

Toby glares at me. "Tess!"

Liv bites her lip. "It's fine, Toby. I get it." There are tears in her eyes.

"Liv, I'm sorry. I just . . ." She pulls the door shut.

Toby turns back on me. "Not cool, Tess."

"It's your fault," I say, pushing my finger into his chest.

"No, it's not," he says calmly, and I hate him for how he can always keep his cool. "You need to go talk to her."

"I know," I say as I rub the back of my neck, begging it to cool down. "But right now, we have bigger problems."

$

Toby and I tear the house apart looking for the money – but find nothing. And we can't ask anybody without giving ourselves away.

"How much do we have on the card?" Toby asks. "Maybe we can give him a bit while we find the rest?"

I check the account online. "Only four hundred and eighty-nine dollars," I sigh. "Don't think that's going to buy us a lot of time."

I lean my head in my hands on the kitchen table. Dad's out with Jake and Dane, Mum's at work, Olivia's in her room (still not talking to me) and Sash is around here somewhere. I have to say, I'm feeling pretty helpless. It's not a feeling I'm familiar with.

Toby puts his hand on my shoulder. "Maybe it's time to tell someone, Tess?"

I look up at him. I know we'll be in so much trouble if we do, but what other option is there? "Maybe you're . . ."

BRING, BRING!

The house phone scares the bejeezus out of me for two reasons. 1) I'm more than a little on edge and 2) that thing never rings. I don't even know why we still have a landline.

I pick up the phone. "Hello?"

"Have you got my money?" I recognise Scotty's voice straightaway. How have I never noticed how creepy it is before now?

"I swear I don't know where it is. If I did, I'd give it back." I can hear that I sound scared. I don't think I've heard my voice sound like that before. I try to shake it off. Toby leans in to listen too.

"Don't give me that crap!" Scotty hisses down the phone at me. "Even a stupid little kid like you can't lose a million dollars. Where is it?"

"I don't know!" Now I can hear myself pleading. I have to pull it together. I mean, What's he going to do, right? If I don't have it, I don't have it.

"You need to listen to me very carefully, kid." Scotty's voice lowers and calms. I find this even scarier. "I'll give you till tomorrow afternoon to get me my money back, or else."

I want to ask, "Or else what?", but I also don't want to know.

"Don't forget, I know where you live. I know where your family lives. I don't know what kind of guy you think I am, but I can tell you now, I'm the bad kind. I'm the kind your parents tell you to stay away from. The kind you should be very scared of."

I know this already. I remember the feeling of his fingers wrapped around my throat.

"And I'm the kind of guy who wants his money back and will do whatever it takes to get it. I have no problem hurting people. So let me make this very clear. Are you listening?"

I'm sure he can hear my panicked breathing over the phone but I manage to squeeze out a squeaky, "Yes."

"I want my money back by tomorrow. All of it. If you tell anyone, and I mean ANYONE – your parents, the cops, even that stupid pet dog of yours – I will come after your family. I know everything about you, Tess, and I know how to get you where it hurts. You have until five p.m. Got it?"

I don't "got it". I have no idea how I'll get him any of his money, let alone all of it. But that's something I'm going to have to work out later. Now, right now, he's threatening my family. It's one thing for me to be in trouble over all of this, but not them. I have no choice but to agree.

"Yes. I got it."

Toby looks at me, shaking his head furiously. But what can I do?

"Five p.m. tomorrow," Scotty spits down the phone and there's a soft click.

I slowly put the phone back on its holder. Toby stares at me wide-eyed and trembles a little. I don't have time for his Chihuahua impression right now.

"But we don't have the money," he says through a quivering bottom lip.

"I know that, Toby."

"How are we going to . . ." His voice trails off.

"I don't know yet. We need to make a plan." I force myself to shake off the terrible feeling bubbling inside of me. Plans are what I do best. It's what *we* do best. We've out-thought our teachers and our parents before, and they all have more smarts in their little toes than Scotty does in his entire evil brain. Surely we can come up with something.

Toby puts his hand on my arm. "We should tell someone. An adult. Maybe your parents or—"

"No," I say sharply. "No adults. They'll tell the police. And you heard what he said. If I tell anyone, he'll come after my family. I won't do that. You're right, we should have told someone earlier, but we didn't and now it's too late. So it's you and me, Toby, like it always is. We have to fix this."

"But this is big, Tess. I don't think you and me is enough."

I don't answer him. Partly because I don't have time to argue. I have a plan to come up with. But mostly because I suspect he may be right. I do think Toby and I can outsmart Scotty, I do. But I also think we'll need help. But it needs to be the right kind of help.

TIP 24

IT'S OK TO ASK FOR HELP.

We don't want to feel like we need help, right? We want to feel strong and smart and independent. And it's not just 'cos we're kids. Even adults need help sometimes, and they don't always want to ask for it. But it's always OK to ask for help from the people you love and trust. You'll see it took me a bit to really understand this, but I thought I'd throw it in here because it's a biggie.

18

Things can only Get ... Worse

We ask for Toby to stay over that night. I'm not going to lie, I'm a little scared, and having someone (even a Toby-someone) sleeping on the floor next to me sounds like a good idea.

At dinner we eat in silence, which has to make Dad a bit suspicious. He tries to start conversations, but Toby and I are "somewhere else" and Olivia's still grumpy. I know I have to talk to her, but with everything that's going on, maybe it's better to have her keep her distance from me for now. Sash is leaning her head against her hand, which I know has a headphone secretly cupped inside. Dane's head is buried in a carpentry magazine, and even Jake seems content chewing on a plate while his dinner sits turned upside down on the table. Mum's at the theatre, of course.

"Wow, so nice to have such a lively family dinner," Dad says sarcastically after his third attempt to start a conversation with little effect. I decide to take my chances.

"Daaad," I say, drawing out his name while I decide how to put what I'm about to say. "I heard at school that the guy next door who got arrested by the police is out again."

Everyone's heads spring up. Except Jake's, he's still chewing.

"What?" says Sash. "You mean he's back next door to us? A murderer, next door?"

"I should build some traps for protection," Dane pipes up. "That way if he ever steps a foot near our house, he'll get strung up like a rabbit."

"He wouldn't hurt us, would he?" says Olivia quietly, cowering a little behind her chicken curry.

"Whoa, whoa, whoa," Dad says, putting both his hands in the air. "Everyone just slow down. Yes, Scotty has managed to get himself released on bail, but you don't need to worry. He's on house arrest at his mum's place in Terret Grove, and isn't allowed anywhere near his place. Or ours!"

He says this in a way that suggests it should be the end to both the conversation and our concern. I don't think so! I look to Toby.

"What's house arrest, Mr Heckleston?" Toby asks quietly. He's trying to sound casual, but he's a terrible actor.

"It's Alik, please, Toby," Dad says. "It means that he can't leave the house, and his mum has to watch him."

"But he *can* leave the house, right?" I say. "I mean, his mum's not gonna stop him."

Dad must have picked up on the concern in my voice. "No, he can't, Tess. He has an ankle monitor, so if he leaves the house the police will know about it and they'll arrest him again."

Toby throws me a confused look and I give him a small shrug.

"How does it work?" I ask.

Dane jumps in. "Haven't you ever seen a cop movie? It's this kind of black cuff that's locked on his ankle with a GPS device inside. The cops set the area that he's allowed in, like his mum's house.

If the ankle device leaves that area, an alarm goes off and the cops can track the device, find him and arrest him. Right, Dad?"

Dad nods.

"Can he turn it off?" I ask.

Dad laughs. "This isn't a James Bond movie. No, he can't turn it off."

"But he can *take* it off," says Sash. She turns her phone towards us. "See, there's like a million videos on YouTube of how to remove an ankle monitor without setting it off."

"Stop it, Sash. Those videos aren't real. It doesn't work like that," says Dad. "Finish your dinner. Scotty isn't coming anywhere near this place."

I poke at my chicken curry. I have a feeling Scotty's probably watched a few YouTube videos in his life.

"I know his mum's house," says Dane. "Butthead and I pass it all the time when we deliver the leaflets. I wonder if I'll get a look at him?"

"You just stay away from that place," warns Dad. "We'll all be fine if we just mind our own business and leave it all to the police. Now, who wants some more curry?"

I look around the table. Nobody has finished their first serving yet – Dad just wants to change the subject. I think maybe I do too.

$

Toby and I don't sleep well that night. We make plans. We throw away plans. We talk about telling someone. We talk about not telling anybody. We have long gaps where we don't talk at all and I wonder if he's fallen asleep.

Then he says, "What if we . . ." and another idea is suggested and discarded.

I get up three times to make sure I've locked the window properly. I guess eventually we sleep, but it's not a good sleep.

I wake up early to find Toby's already awake and scribbling in his notebook.

"What are you doing?" I say.

He chews on his pen. "Just more ideas."

"Any good ones?"

He shakes his head.

I get up and go to the window again. It's still locked. I gaze out into the garden. At the washing line where Dane strung Butthead up by a carabiner as Olivia giggled uncontrollably and Dane shouted, "Dog-Pan!" At the trampoline where I jumped and watched Scotty over the fence when I should have minded my own business. At my treasure chest, where I found the . . . My breath catches.

"Toby," I say, but it's more of a whisper because my voice is stuck in my throat.

"Yeah?"

I wave him over. Toby stands next to me and I point down to the garden. There on my treasure chest sits a can of soft drink with a twenty tucked into it. We look at each other, and run downstairs without a word.

I knock the can aside and open the lid of the chest. It's empty except for a yellow envelope. I don't think I want to know what's inside, but I force my hand to reach in and take it. As Toby peers over my shoulder, I pull out a piece of notepaper and what looks like a page from a newspaper. I unfold the note first. It reads:

MAYBE SHE KNOWS WHERE THE
MONEY IS? 5P.M. TODAY.

I can't make sense of the message, but my hands shake a little as I unfold the newspaper article. There, staring back at me, is the picture of Kooky Kathy. She's beaming at the camera, shaking hands with the Guide Dog man. Just my luck, Scotty is the only person in Watterson who reads this stupid paper.

Toby makes a small whimpering sound in my ear. "Kathy!" he says. "Scotty has Kathy."

We tear through the house, ignoring Dad's insistence that we "slow down and have some breakfast".

"We'll be back in a sec, Dad. We'll have something then!" I call as we pull on our shoes.

"Where are you going?" he insists.

"Just to Brennan Park. Early morning walk. Fresh air and all that," I say, hoping he will just drop it.

"OK, but make sure you eat when you get back," he says.

Toby and I sprint to Brennan Park and down to the Lego house. We bang on the wall.

"Kathy! Kathy!" Toby shouts. He's starting to panic. I am too, but I'm trying not to show it. "What if he has her? What if he's hurt her?"

A thick feeling of guilt starts to swirl in my belly and rise up to my throat. I've only vomited once before, when I had some weird stomach bug in Year Three, but it felt a little like this. Can you vomit from guilt?

Then I hear a sound that pushes the feeling right back down again. It's "Three Little Birds" by Bob Marley, sung slightly out of key. We duck around behind the Lego house and there, on the bench underneath a huge jacaranda tree, Kathy is sitting cross-legged, strumming her guitar. Her terrible singing has never sounded so good.

I squeeze Toby's shoulder as we walk over to her. "Elvis. Lennon. You two look highly strung. All that money not making you happy?" She smiles a knowing smile at us and although I'm glad she's OK, I'm not a big fan of that smile. It feels like an "I told you so" smile. She quickly switches her song to "I Can't Get No Satisfaction", and I try to ignore the irony.

Toby gives her an awkward hug. It squishes the guitar between them but Kathy doesn't seem to mind.

"We're so glad you're OK!" he says.

"Why wouldn't I be OK?" she asks.

"It's just that . . . well, we thought . . ." Toby looks at me.

I pause. Scotty said not to tell anyone. But who's Kooky Kathy going to tell, right? And she already knows about the money. I feel like maybe if we have someone else to talk to, it might help us work out what to do. I won't tell her everything, just enough to get some advice.

"Well," I begin. "So you know that money . . ."

Before I know it, it's like someone has turned on a tap and I can't turn it off. My dad would call it 'verbal diarrhoea'. The story gushes out of me like it's wanted to be free for a long time. Every detail. From the first twenty dollars Scotty gave me, to the newspaper article in the treasure chest and the panicked sprint to the park. And when I finish, I feel lighter somehow.

"Well, you've certainly got yourself into a bit of a pickle, haven't you?" Kathy says as she plucks a few notes on the guitar.

"So what do you think we should do?" Toby asks.

"How would I know?" says Kathy.

Toby and I stare at each other. Adults always tell you what you should do. That's what they're there for, right? I mean, it's their job. I know Kathy's kind of out there, but she's still an adult.

"Do you think we should tell someone?" Toby asks.

"He said you can't, or else he'd hurt your family," Kathy answers unhelpfully.

"You think we should have told someone about the money when we first found it, don't you?" I say.

"Coulda, shoulda, woulda. It's a bit late for that, isn't it?" Kathy leans on her guitar. "You can't change the past, so you have to find solutions for the future."

I'm finding her riddles particularly annoying today.

"Look, you two are the smartest kids I know. You're probably the smartest people I know. Me? I live in a park. I've made more mistakes than anyone. So I'm not going to tell you what you should do. I don't even tell Mr Piddles what to do."

"But we don't know," I say, admitting it out loud for the first time. "We need help."

"Then get help," Kathy says.

"From who?" Toby asks.

"From other smart people. From people who you trust. People who have your back. People who care about the same things as you. Everybody's got their people. And you've gotta help your people."

My jaw clenches. "Rrrr, I don't care about your riddles, Kathy. Right now, I just care that my family is safe." Kathy just nods and goes back to her guitar. She strums a few chords and starts to sing "We are Family" by Sister Sledge.

I grab Toby's hand and pull him away. I feel annoyed that I was so concerned about Kathy. She's no help at all.

$

I push open our squeaky front gate and we head down the path overgrown with weeds.

"Hey, Tess? I'm really glad Kathy's OK, but Scotty's note doesn't really make sense, right?

I mean, he must have known we'd go check on her and know it was an empty threat."

"Yeah," I mutter. Toby's right. He's totally right. But I'm trying to push that feeling away.

As we walk back into the house Dad's just getting off his phone. He's frowning and doesn't pounce on us about eating breakfast.

"You OK, Dad?" I ask.

"Yeah, I'm fine," he says unconvincingly. "It's just, your mum went to the theatre this morning to open up for a technician to come fix the lights. He's there now, but no one's there to let him in. And your mum's not answering her phone." He tries to shrug off any concern. "I'm sure she's just picking up something for the show and she'll be back soon."

I stop in the hall. The vomit feeling comes back. I pull the newspaper article out of my pocket and unfold it. Under the picture of Kathy it reads . . .

GENEROUS LOCAL THEATRE MANAGER
JENNIFER HECKLESTON DONATES $1000
TO GUIDE DOG FUNDRAISER.

The vomit feeling reaches my throat and sits there, threatening to spill forward as I squeeze out the words . . .

"Toby. Scotty doesn't have Kathy. He has my mum."

In that second, everything changes. I'm not scared any more. I. AM. MAD!

19

No More Nice Tess

TIP 25

CHANNEL YOUR ANGER.

It's OK to get angry. Sometimes things suck.
We always get told to "calm down". Forget that!
Angry people take action. Angry people change
things. Have you seen Greta Thunberg's
speech to the United Nations? WATCH IT!
She's angry. And she's awesome. Take your
anger and do something with it.

BRING, BRING!

The landline rings again, but this time I don't jump. This time I'm not scared.

"Don't bother answering it," Dad says. "It's been ringing all morning, but when I pick up no one's there. Probably telemarketers." He walks out of the kitchen and I grab the phone.

"Do you have my mum?" I say, trying to sound calm while I can almost feel steam rising from the top of my head.

Scotty laughs. I hate that laugh. "Yes," he says. "Do you have my money?"

"Yes," I answer without hesitating. Toby stares at me, his mouth dropping open.

"Well then, we no longer have a problem, do we?"

"Is she OK?"

"She's fine. And she'll stay fine as long as I get my money by five p.m."

"OK. Where should we meet you?"

"At Balthazar Theatre. I guess you know it, right?"

"I do. You'd better not hurt her."

"And you'd better have every cent of my money, or you can say goodbye to your mummy."

I take a deep breath to calm myself. "It will all be there. But, Scotty?"

"What?"

"I'm ten years old. I don't call her 'Mummy'." I slam down the phone.

I must look pretty furious, because Toby's nervous about his next question.

"Uh, Tess, how are we going to find a million dollars by five o'clock?"

"I don't know, Toby. But you and I are going to figure it out."

Toby looks at his watch. "But it's already eleven a.m. We don't have a lot of time."

"You're right," I say. "We're going to need some help."

"You're going to tell an adult?" Toby asks in disbelief.

I laugh. "Of course not! I said we need help. Adults aren't any good for that." I wink at Toby then grab his arm and drag him out the front.

Dane's on the lawn, working on some huge contraption as Butthead barks at a bird up a tree.

"Dane! Heckleston Huddle. Now!"

He looks up from the complicated knot he's trying to tie. "What? We haven't had one of those in years."

"Well, we're having one now. Five minutes. My room."

"But—"

"Dane. Please."

He sighs and starts to pack his stuff away. I take that as a yes and head upstairs. I push open Sash's door.

"Hey!" she says as I burst into her room. "Knocking!"

"Sorry, Sash, but this is an emergency. Heckleston Huddle. My room. Now."

Sash rolls her eyes. Is that where I got it from?

"We're not little kids any more, Tess. There's no biscuit jar to raid."

"Sash, when's the last time I asked you for anything?"

She actually has to think about this. Even I can't remember, but it must be years. She shrugs.

"Right. So now I'm asking you. Please. My room. Five minutes."

Her eyes roll again. But then she reaches up and takes out her earphones. It's a miracle! She coming AND she's coming unplugged. Toby and I head up to my room.

"Tess?"

I stop. Olivia stands at her door, peering through the opening. "Do you need me too?"

She must have heard me with Sash. "Um, no. It's OK, Liv. Just go back into your room and rest. We've got some stuff to talk about. Boring stuff."

I expect some kind of argument, but Olivia just nods her head slowly and goes back into her room. She's still upset with me – and fair enough – but I don't have time to worry about that now. We have some serious planning to do.

$

Now that I have Sash and Dane here, sitting in a circle on my bedroom floor like you would round a campfire, I'm not sure where to start. I can see Sash reaching for her earphones and I know I don't have long before I lose her into plugged-world.

"Mum's been kidnapped!" I blurt out. Toby stares at me.

"Not exactly how I would have eased into the story," he says.

Dane snorts and Sash looks at me like I'm mad. "Yeah right!" she says. "Who would want to kidnap *our* mum? And for what ransom? A second helping of Dad's stroganoff?"

Dad's stroganoff is pretty awesome, but that's not important right now.

"Scotty kidnapped her."

Dane and Sash pause. The mention of the only bad guy we know just bought some possible credibility to my story.

"What are you talking about?" Dane says slowly.

"I think you'd better start from the beginning, Tess," Toby says. "And tell them everything. They can't help if they don't know everything."

And so I do. I tell them everything. And when I finish they're doing that goldfish thing – mouth open, eyes blinking, not saying anything.

I wait. And wait.

Then Dane's goldfish mouth curls up at the sides and turns into a smile.

"Dude! You're in SOOOOOO much trouble!" And he laughs. Our mum is kidnapped, I have to conjure a million dollars out of thin air, and he's laughing. Toby sniggers. I glare at him.

"He's right," Toby says. "You're in so, so, SO much trouble."

Sash joins in. "Like dead meat. Like grounded for-evs."

I laugh a little too. It's a manic kind of laugh – I know I've got nothing to laugh about. But it feels good. And as we sit there on my bedroom floor, laughing at my misfortune, I know I made the right decision. These are the people who are going to help me make this right. These are *my* people. We're going to save Mum and bring that dirtbag Scotty down!

"OK, fine. Now that we've all had a good laugh at my expense, can we please come up with some kind of plan?" I look at my watch. "We only have five hours left."

Toby gets out his notebook. "List time!" he says, and everyone's ready to get down to business. "What do we need?"

"A million dollars," says Sash.

"And how are we gonna get it?" asks Dane.

"I might have an idea for that one," says Toby. "It's not going to be a solution, but it might give us enough time to get your mum back."

I remember when we were younger, we used to sit around like this and plan out our Saturday adventures. We haven't done this for a long time. Too long. It's funny how you can sort of miss your family, even when you're with them every day. Well, I miss this.

And so, there on the floor of my bedroom, Sash, Dane, Toby and I make a plan. Not just any plan. Not a plan to make us a few dollars. A plan that will get our mum back. The most important plan we've ever made.

TIP 26

FOUR HEADS ARE BETTER THAN ONE.

No matter how clever you are, you can't be the cleverest at everything. When you get other people involved in something they'll bring different ideas, different points of view, different talents to the table. If you can't solve a problem on your own, get some other brains involved.

20

Plan of Attack

Within an hour everyone has their assigned jobs and we're ready to kick our plan into action.

"All right," I say. "We meet back here at four. We need to be at the theatre by four thirty to make sure we're there before Scotty. Any questions?"

Everyone shakes their heads.

"I feel like we should all put our hands together and shout 'GO TEAM!' or something," says Toby.

"That's dumb," says Sash.

"Totally dumb," I say.

"Pfft, yeah," agrees Dane.

Toby smiles. "Wanna do it anyway?" He puts his hand out. We all put our hands on top.

"GO TEAM!" We throw our hands in the air.

"See? Dumb," says Sash. But she's smiling.

"We're going out!" Sash calls to Dad.

He sticks his head out of the kitchen. His shirt is covered in food, so I guess he's feeding Jake. "All of you?" he says, surprised. "Together?"

"Yeah," says Dane like it's something that happens every day. It's not.

Dad raises his eyebrows. "Um, OK. Don't be too long. Sash, you're in charge."

"Does that mean it's you that'll get grounded for-evs?" I say under my breath.

"You wish!" she says.

We go outside and jump on our scooters. I pop one of my earphones in and pick a song on my MP3 player. We split up and head off in different directions. The perfect soundtrack plays as I push my foot along the pavement – "We're Not Gonna Take It" by Twisted Sister.

$

I peer over Toby's shoulder as he zips the mouse across the screen. We're at his mums' print shop.

Toby helps out a lot at Copy Cats and is a whiz with all this stuff. I often watch him put together a flyer for us from bits and pieces of things he's found on the internet, rearranging them and adding text and borders and changing the colour. Within minutes, he can create something that looks like a professional magazine ad. Without Toby, I'd be scribbling things on cardboard with a marker pen.

But today he's concentrating intensely on a very different project. On the computer screen in front of him are images of different bank notes – hundreds, fifties, twenties – which he's duplicating and moving into rows. On another page, he has the backside of the notes. He's lining them up as they snap to little red guidelines on the screen. I really have no idea how he's doing it all, but what I *do* know is that the money on the screen looks pretty real. Definitely the kind of real that could fool an idiot like Scotty.

"It looks great, Toby, but when we print it on paper it won't feel real, right?" I say.

Toby scoots the mouse back and forth, not taking his eyes off the screen. The notes shuffle around and zoom in and out as he slightly adjusts the colour. "I'm not going to print it on paper," he mumbles, concentrating. "I'm going to print it on clear polymer."

He says it like I'm supposed to have a clue what he's talking about. Toby knows a lot about paper and printing. He's always telling me A4 this and B5 that, 300gsm something with a spot gloss whatever. It's all blah, blah, blah to me, but Toby knows what he's talking about.

My silence must clue him in. "It's a plasticky paper that feels like money," he explains. "I'll do double sided A0 prints. Three lines of hundreds, one of each of fifties and twenties. Sixteen notes per line. That's five thousand, nine hundred and twenty dollars per page so we need a hundred and seventy runs. I've set up the auto trimmer to these guides so we'll have a million fake dollars in no time."

I pretty much only understand the last bit of what he said. But it's the only bit that really counts. Toby, my best friend, is single-handedly solving the first problem on our list.

1) Get one million dollars for the ransom

It's at this point in time I'd like to refer you back to **Tip 2: Get a best friend like Toby**! Having a Toby is the best.

We've offered to watch the shop for an hour while Toby's mums go and have lunch together, so we have the place to ourselves. It's super-quiet on Sundays anyway – his mums just use it as an opportunity to catch up on the week's jobs. Before I know it, Toby has pressed "send" and the printer whirs to life and starts churning. If you've never been in a proper print shop before, commercial printers are nothing like your little laser printer at home. They're these giant machines, like some futuristic T-rex come to life, swallowing up plain paper and spitting out colourful prints. I run over to the other side of the printer and watch as it spews out the first sheet, then sucks it back in to print the other side. Page after page of our fake banknotes flop on top of each other. And they look so good. As I breathe in the warm smell of the freshly printed sheets, I'm feeling good about our plan.

Toby and I grab the giant pieces of paper and carry them over to the trimmer. He feeds the first one through to make sure he's lined up the cutting guides properly. Our first pile of fake money is sliced up. We pick up a hundred-dollar note each and turn it over in our fingers.

"It's pretty good," I say.

Toby nods. "It will definitely buy us some time. We can't give him too long with it, though. If he looks too closely, he'll see it's fake. But a big pile of it in a bag – it should be enough to get your mum back."

"For sure," I say, nodding thoughtfully and rolling the note over. "Don't take this the wrong way, but I'm a little surprised. Counterfeit money feels more like a Tess idea than a Toby idea."

"It's more just a prop, really. I mean, we're not going to try to spend it – no real business would take it anyway. But in a dark theatre with a guy like Scotty . . . well, we just need something to buy us some time."

I give Toby a small smile. "Sounds like I might be rubbing off on you after all."

He shakes his head. "I really hope not."

"Me too," I say. "But thanks. I couldn't get Mum back without your help. I know I'm not always the best friend, but you are."

Toby gives me a quick hug and I don't push him away.

Then he hands me the first pile of fake money.

"All right. I'll trim up the rest and you start scrunching it. Try to make it look less new, and then chuck it into bundles. There are rubber bands over there."

We get to work and before Toby's mums get back from lunch, we have our bag of one million fake dollars ready to go.

We're back at the house before four. Sash is already there, plugged and clicking away furiously on her laptop. She gives us a quick thumbs-up as we walk into the lounge. I nod back. The bag of printed money has been stashed behind the hedge in the front garden so Dad doesn't spot it. Dane comes bursting through the front door covered in dust and sweat with all kinds of gadgets dangling from his tool belt. He has a bit of an Indiana Jones thing going on. If you haven't seen any of the Indiana Jones movies, skip Google and go straight to iTunes and download them. Best movies ever!

Dane gives us a nod. "All set!" Butthead comes trotting in behind him, head in the air proudly, tail wagging and BAM! He runs straight into Dane's leg. I shake my head at him.

"Hey," Dane says. "He's not as silly as he looks, you know."

"Sure thing. Total Wonderdog, that one."

Dane bends down to give Butthead a pat. "You don't listen to her," he says in a baby-doggy voice.

"We all good?" I ask. Dane, Sash and Toby nod in unison and I head into the kitchen. Dad's stacking the dishwasher, Jake's chewing on the chair leg and Olivia's colouring in at the kitchen table.

"Hey, Dad," I say, trying to act as casual as possible. "Me and Dane and Sash were thinking about going to The Funky Anchovy for some pizza and ice cream."

Dad tries to cram the last of the dishes into the already full machine. "But I'm making nasi goreng tonight. And we had takeaway last week."

"It's OK, we're going to pay. We saved up. Please, Dad."

Dad stops and looks up. "Can I come?"

I pause. "We were kind of thinking just us kids. You know, a sort of sibling bonding thing."

Dad's eyebrows raise. "Sibling bonding? Who are you? And what have you done with my kids?" I try to laugh it off. "All right, it's your money, and your loss, missing out on my nasi goreng. Are you taking Liv?"

I freeze and look at Olivia. I hadn't thought this part through. How do I convince him that one sibling shouldn't come for the sibling bonding outing? Liv looks up at me and gives me a sort of sideways smile. It's hard to read, but it feels like she knows I don't want her to come. And yep, there they are again, those pangs of guilt swirling in my gut. Before I can say anything, Olivia turns to Dad.

"It's OK, Dad, I can't eat anything there anyway. Plus, I'd hate to miss out on your nasi goreng."

Dad scruffs her hair. "That's my girl. At least someone appreciates my culinary flair."

Olivia looks at me and gives me that weird smile again, then goes back to her colouring.

"So we can go?" I say.

"Yeah, OK. But be home before eight. And can you swing past the theatre on the way and check on your mum? She's still not answering her phone."

"You know what she's like, Dad. She probably forgot to turn the thing on. Or left it in the costume room."

"Yeah, I know, but just tell her to call me anyway. And tell her it's called a mobile phone because you're supposed to take it *with* you."

"Sure, Dad. Thanks. See you, Liv."

Olivia doesn't look up as the four of us head out of the house, grab the bag and head to Mum's theatre.

21

Balthazar Theatre

Obviously, we're not going for pizza. But The Funky Anchovy is pretty much opposite the theatre, so it's a perfect decoy. Dane says he needs to take a little detour and heads off somewhere, but the rest of us arrive at the theatre way ahead of time. We split up and head to our designated spots: Sash to the AV booth and Toby and me to the dress circle. We've picked spots where we have a good view of the entrance and Scotty when he comes in, but far enough away from him to be safe. The theatre's dark despite it still being day. It's part of the magic of the place, really. It doesn't matter what's happening outside – you step in here and you're transported to another place, another time, another world.

The production of *Peter Pan* starts next week, so right now the theatre has what Mum calls down-days. It's the few days between the end of one show and the start of another. It essentially means the place is a mess. All the sets from the last show (which was *Dracula*) are still lying around while the *Peter Pan* sets are going up. It gives the place a spooky, crossbred feel. I really don't need spooky right now.

I pull out the shiny new walkie-talkie. We decided this was the perfect investment for our last four hundred dollars. Dane made sure we got the good kind with the long reach and the earpieces, so I'm feeling pretty professional. I can almost hear "Playing to Win" by Little River Band playing as I press the button.

"Sash, can we get a bit of light? Maybe just in the aisle?" I whisper into the walkie-talkie.

"Roger that, sis," Sash's voice crackles through. The lower level intermission lights slowly fade up.

Now we can see everything on the theatre floor below, but it's still dark where we are. The perfect incognito bird's-eye view. Incognito is an Italian word meaning "staying concealed". It was also a British acid jazz band in the 80s. Maybe don't Google them because they weren't great . . . but it's a really cool word.

The walkie-talkie crackles again with Dane's voice. "Hey guys, I'm here. Heading straight up to the catwalk." The catwalk is a little walkway that runs through the roof of the theatre, between all the lighting trusses. It's there so the lighting engineer or set designers can get up to change the lights or install something. Dane pretty much spent his entire childhood up there with the rigging guys. I watch him as he scampers up the ladder and along the platform in the dark, looking more like a sure-footed Spiderman than the doofus of a big brother I know. He disappears into the shadows. I guess Dane's made the wise decision to leave Butthead outside, which I'm grateful for. That dog would be sure to mess things up.

Dane's voice crackles back through the earpiece, "OK, Tess, so see that square on the floor below?" I look down and see where Dane has marked out a square using gaffer tape. It's on the ground in the aisle and right below the dress circle – exactly where Scotty will have to stand to see me.

"Yep!" I reply.

"OK, so I have five sandbag traps set up above that square. As long as you keep him there, I can take him out with the pull of a rope," Dane explains.

"Got it. Sash, can you narrow the lights a bit so that's the only area that's not dark?"

"No problem," Sash answers, and the lights adjust to the square.

"Perfect," I say. "Now, Dane, knocking him out with a sandbag is a last resort, OK? We want to get in and out of this with as little hassle as possible. Don't do *anything* unless I give the word."

"Aw man!" Dane complains. "I really wanna see my sandbag smack-down in action."

"Not without my word!"

"Fine," Dane says. "Over and out."

And so there we wait, in the dark, quiet theatre. Weirdly, I wish Scotty would hurry up. This waiting is giving me too much time to think about stuff I don't want to think about.

1) What if he's hurt Mum?
2) What if the fake money doesn't work?
3) What if he has backup?
4) What if he takes us all hostage?

I take a deep breath and answer my own illogical questions logically.

1) He wouldn't hurt Mum. She's his bargaining tool.
2) The fake money only has to work long enough to get Mum back.
3) He won't have backup. He won't want anyone else to know what's going on. Plus, he probably doesn't have any friends after the whole police raid and jail thing.
4) There's just one of him and there are four of us. Plus, he's a bad guy and we're good kids.

218

I've seen enough movies to know the good kids win.

But I'm not the good kid, am I?

I mean, I took a million dollars that wasn't mine. I put my sister in hospital, I got my mum kidnapped and I dragged my best friend and my brother and sister into this mess.

I know Scotty's the bad guy, that's for sure. But I'm not sure that I'm the good guy. I rack my brains to think of a movie where the "less bad guy" wins. Nothing. Before I have time to panic, the theatre door swings open and a figure walks in.

I know that walk. I know that greasy hair shining in the theatre lights. I know that raspy breath. Scotty strides into the theatre and stops in the middle of the aisle, right on Dane's sandbag square. I'm sure Dane's itching to pull the rope right this second. Sash chucks the spot on, lighting him up.

Scotty throws his hand up to his eyes and squints blindly into the seating above him.

The bad guy is here. It's showtime!

22

The Showdown

TIP 27

DON'T UNDERESTIMATE PEOPLE.
I talked about this a bit in **Tip 3** – about how adults
can underestimate kids. But It's not just adults
that do it. Everybody does. it's a big mistake. Every
single person you meet in your life has the poten-
tial to be better, smarter, stronger and braver
than you, in every single way. Be ready for it.

"All right, Tess," Scotty snarls. "Where are you?
You'd better have my money."

"Up here!" I call. Sash backs the spotlight off a little so Scotty can see Toby and I up in the dress circle.

"Who's that? I thought I told you to come alone."

"He's my best friend. He found the money with me. He's not telling anyone."

Toby lifts the bag of fake money into the air and a smile peels through Scotty's thin lips.

"Is that what I think it is?" he says.

"Yep," I say. "Every cent. But first, where's my mum?" Toby drops the bag back down to his feet. Scotty glares up at us.

"Give me the money, and I'll give you your mum."

Toby leans in. "No way, Tess," he whispers. "If he sees the money's fake, there's no way we'll get her back."

I nod. "No! What's saying you won't take the money and run? I want Mum first. Then you'll get your money."

Scotty stabs his finger towards us. "Don't try to bargain with me, kid. Throw the money down now, or your mum will pay for it."

"Give him this."

Toby and I whip around to face the voice behind us. In the shadows of the dress circle stands Olivia, clutching something to her chest.

"Olivia!" I whisper-shout. "What are you doing here?"

"I followed you. I know what's going on. You may not want to include me in a Heckleston Huddle, but I'm a Heckleston, Tess. There's no stopping me listening in at the door."

Scotty shouts from down below. "What's going on? I want my money!"

Olivia gives me a nervous smile. "Give him this," she repeats.

She throws something towards me. I catch it and look down. It's money. Not fake, printed-at-Toby's-mums'-shop money but real, cold-hard-cash money. It must be at least ten thousand.

My mouth drops open like a goldfish. "Where did you get this?"

"Toby's backpack," she says. "I guess when you're a millionaire it's easy to lose track of little bit like this, huh?"

I turn on Toby. "Seriously? Mister Account Keeper? Mister 'I keep track of every cent of the money'? Didn't think this would come in handy?"

It's Toby's turn to do a goldfish impression. "What? I . . . no . . . it's . . . I . . ."

Scotty's getting impatient. "If you kids don't give me my money right now, you can say goodbye to your mum."

Olivia grabs my arm. "Throw it down to him. Tell him he'll get the rest after he lets Mum go."

There's not much else to do but follow my seven-year-old sister's orders. Yup, this feels weird.

"Stay back," I instruct Olivia as I move over to the railing. I toss the money down to Scotty.

"Here. This is a down payment. Let Mum go and you can have the rest. I promise. I don't want it, anyway. It's caused me too much trouble. I just want Mum back. Let her go and you can have it all."

Scotty turns the money over in his hands. He fans through the notes as he thinks it over. Finally he looks up, his mouth curling at the edges in a snarl.

"OK, kid. You've got yourself a deal."

"So where is she?" I demand.

"Well," Scotty scoffs, "funny thing is, she's been here all along. I didn't so much kidnap her as lock her in the props basement while she was tidying up this morning. So all ya gotta do is go down and unlock the door."

"You mean she doesn't even know she's been kidnapped?" I ask.

"Nup." Scotty runs a hand through his greasy hair. "You think I want to add kidnapping to my rap sheet? I'm in enough trouble with the cops already. I just want my money back."

I turn to Toby. "What do we do?"

"I guess one of us has to let her out, and try to get her out of here without her seeing any of us."

"I'm not going! She'll want to go home together, and I'm not leaving you here to deal with him." I poke my finger down at Scotty.

"Well, I'm not leaving *you* here," says Toby.

"I'll go," Olivia says softly.

"What?" Toby and I turn to her.

"I'll go get Mum. I'll tell her I came looking for her when she didn't answer Dad's calls. She'll want to take me home straightaway, leaving you to deal with Scotty. Plus, Dad will forgive me for sneaking out because I'll just say I was really, really worried about Mummy." Olivia clasps her hands in front of her chest, sticks out her bottom lip and stares up at me with her best puppy-dog eyes.

"Wow, you're good," I say.

"I learnt from the best," she says with a grin.

"OK." I bend down, putting both my hands on her shoulders. "Go get Mum, and get her out of here without her seeing any of us."

"Too easy!" Olivia says.

"And Liv . . ."

"Yeah?"

"Thanks. We couldn't have done this without you."

"I know that," she says. "Just remember it next time, OK?"

"You bet," I say and watch my little sister head down the dress circle staircase.

I lean over the railing and call down to Scotty. "I'm sending my sister to let Mum out."

He glares at me. "Your sister? How many of you are up there? I told you to come alone."

"Look, do you want your money? Do you want to walk out of here without getting the police involved? Then shut up, hide and stay hidden. If Mum sees any of us, we're all busted."

"Who do you think you're talking to, you little brat? If you don't . . ."

"Muuuuum?" Olivia calls out at the top of her voice. The staircase comes down to the middle of the theatre floor, so she's standing in a face-off with Scotty. He glares at her. "I'm going to find my mum now," she says, glaring back at him. "Mum and me can walk out of the theatre together or we can call the police together. Up to you."

As I watch from the balcony, I have my finger on the walkie-talkie button, ready to give Dane the go to drop a sandbag on Scotty's head if he takes one step towards Liv.

Scotty hesitates. He gives a small growl and then slips into the shadows of the seating. Toby and I move back in the dress circle and Sash turns off the spotlight. With this low lighting, Olivia should be able to walk Mum straight through the theatre without her seeing any of us. We hold our breath and wait.

"Mum? Muuuuuum?" Olivia cries as she heads towards the props basement. It's a sort of trapdoor that opens up onto some stairs that lead down to a room under the theatre. It's dark and creepy, and I feel pretty bad for Mum that she's spent the whole day down there. Muffled cries can be heard from below the trapdoor.

"Mum? Mum, are you in there?" Olivia calls. She's really playing the part well. I hear the slide of a lock and a creak as Liv lifts the trapdoor open. Out rushes Mum, and Olivia disappears into her hug.

"Liv! Thank you! Thank you! Thank you! I've been stuck down there all day and there's no phone reception because this theatre was built a million years ago. How did you find me? Is your dad here?" Mum rushes Liv out onto the stage and looks around. She strains her eyes to peer into the dark theatre as we all shrink back against walls and into shadows.

"Um. No, Dad's at home," says Olivia.

"What?" says Mum. "He let you come here alone? It's so dark. Let's get some lights on and I'll finish a few things and we can go home." Mum feels her way along the wall of the stage wings. I know what she searching for – the house lights! If she switches those on the whole place will light up like a Christmas tree.

"Mum, let's just go, ок?" begs Olivia.

"What are you talking about? We can hardly see where we're walking. The lights are here some-where. Just hang on." Mum slides her hand further along the wall towards the switch. We're all about to get totally busted. She swipes up and down, centimetres from the switch. "If Dad's at home, who did you come here with?"

"After you get what you want, you don't want it."

Mum stops and spins around to face Kooky Kathy standing centre stage, Mr Piddles perched proudly on her shoulder. She's strumming her guitar and singing loudly to an imaginary audience.

"If I gave you the moon, you'd grow tired of it soon," Kathy sings as she glides across the stage.

It's the first time I've ever heard her sing in tune. I have to say, she's not that bad. She's no Aretha Franklin, but she's not bad. And most importantly, Mum's forgotten about the house lights.

"You're always wishing and wanting for something. When you get what you want, you don't want what you get," Kathy's voice carries to the back of the theatre as she spins on the stage. She doesn't look so kooky right now. She looks kind of . . . beautiful.

"'Cos after you get what you want, you don't want what you wanted at all. I know youuuuuuuu!"

I stop myself from bursting into a round of applause, but Olivia doesn't. She claps as Kathy bows dramatically to the empty theatre. Mum snaps out of her trance.

"Kathy, hon, what are you doing here?" Mum asks.

"Oh, I've always wanted to be in the theatre!" Kathy says, waving her hand flamboyantly in front of her. "And I feel like this was my moment."

"But how did you get in here? I mean—"

"She brought me," Olivia jumps in. "I mean, you didn't think I came alone, right? Dad's watching Jake, so Kathy brought me."

"Oh, thank you, Kathy," Mum gushes. "That's so kind of you."

"Of course," says Kathy. "Like I always say, you gotta help your people." Kathy turns to look up at Toby and me hiding in the shadows and winks.

"Let's go home, Mum," says Olivia. "Dad's waiting for you. We've all been waiting for you."

Mum kisses Olivia's head and gives her a squeeze. "OK, Liv. I've missed the electrician and won't be able to get him back out until tomorrow anyhow. Plus, I'm starving after being locked up all day. I could really do with some of your dad's cooking. Come on, Kathy, we'll drop you off on the way."

"Or maybe she could come over for dinner?" says Olivia, sliding her hand into Kathy's. "Dad made nasi goreng."

"That's a great idea, Liv," says Mum, taking her other hand.

Olivia, Mum and Kathy head down the aisle and push open the doors. Just as they leave I hear Mum say to Kathy, "Your hair looks really great, Kathy, I wonder if we use the same hairdresser."

"That's highly likely," says Kathy as they close the doors behind them.

$

"All right, you little brats. You've got your mum, now give me my money," Scotty calls as he steps back into the middle of the theatre.

"OK, it's coming." I pick up the bag and whisper to Toby. "I'll throw the bag over and then we run, OK? Don't take the stairs, they go straight to the theatre floor and smack-bang into Scotty. Take the rigging ladder – it leads to the side emergency exit. I broke the tag off the bag zipper, so it'll take him a bit to open it and maybe buy us some time. Whatever happens, don't stop. I'll be right behind you."

Toby nods. I move to the balcony railing and hold the sports bag over the edge. "Here's your money," I say. "Now, why don't you take it and crawl back into whatever hole you came from?"

Scotty reaches up with his tattooed hands. "Yeah, OK, kid. Nice tough guy speech. Why don't you shut up and give me the money before I come up there and take it?"

"Three, two, one, go!" I throw the bag and run. Toby's in front and I don't think I've ever seen him move so fast. He reaches the ladder first and down he goes. He hits the floor and heads for the side door. I scoot down the ladder after him. Just before my feet touch the floor – YOINK!

"Where do you think you're going so fast?" Scotty grabs me and yanks me off the rungs. My feet are dangling just above the ground like they're still trying to climb down the ladder. I see Toby freeze at the door and turn round.

"Don't you want to wait around while I count it and make sure it's all there?" Scotty says. Toby's still frozen at the door. He's starting to shake – more than his usual Chihuahua thing. He looks seriously scared.

"Just go!" I mouth to him.

For a second he looks like he might, but then he shakes his head. "You're my people," he says.

"So, I have an idea," Scotty spits in my ear. "I'm gonna stay here and keep a hold of you while your little friend opens the bag and counts the money in front of me. Once we're sure it's all there, then everyone can be on their way. Sound good?"

My feet are still not touching the ground, so I don't really see how I have much choice in the matter. Toby manages a nod despite the shaking.

"OK, great!" says Scotty. Using his foot, he kicks the bag over to Toby. "Start counting, kid, and no funny business, or your little friend here might find herself in a whole lotta hurt. Got it?"

Toby nods and bends down. Pinching the broken zip between his nails, he opens the bag and pulls out the piles of fake money. Scotty and I are a couple of metres away from Toby and it's still pretty dark, so I'm crossing my fingers and toes that Scotty won't be able to tell that the money's not real. Toby starts to count it.

"Out loud!" Scotty orders.

"Five hundred, six hundred, seven hundred . . ."

I know how long it takes to count this much money, which gives me time to think. Except that I'm coming up blank. I look over my shoulder to see Dane's sandbag drop zone a metre or so away from us. No chance he's coming to the rescue. Do I just play it cool, hoping that Scotty takes the money and lets us leave? It's nice to think that might happen, but it's also unlikely. He'll check the money. He will. He's not exactly the trusting type. I need help, but my earpiece has been knocked out and is dangling unhelpfully from my shirt. I'm pinned against Scotty's chest, feet barely touching the ground, arms flailing. It's official. I'm useless.

"Eight thousand two hundred, eight thousand three hundred . . ."

"OK, fine," says Scotty. "Do it in thousands, I don't have all day."

Toby nods again. But as he bends back down to the money I see him look up. It's a quick look but I see it. He continues to count under his breath, saying out loud every thousand he puts down. But when I look closer he's not counting the hundreds in between, he's talking. He still has his earpiece in. I try to look up without moving my head and see a shape creep silently above us. Toby continues to nod-whisper-count. Something slides behind him. It's too dark to see what it is. As Toby grabs the next pile of money from the bag, I see a small slip of the hand as he reaches behind his back. What has he got?

After what seems like an eternity of counting, Toby gets to a million. "There," he says. "It's all there. You can let her go now."

"I'll let her go when I'm ready," Scotty says and moves towards Toby, still clinging to me tightly. "Now, pass her the bag slowly. We'll take it to my car and once both me and the money are safely inside, I'll let her go. So don't try anything stupid."

Toby passes me the bag with two hands. As my hand touches his, he pushes something cold and metal into it. I can't see very well, but I recognise the shape. It's a carabiner.

"Dane says 'Dog-Pan'," Toby whispers.

"What?" Scotty spits at him. "What did you say?"

I roll the carabiner around in my hand and nod. "He said 'DOG-PAN!'"

Sash cranks the lights and blares music from the speakers. Scotty spins around frantically and I take my opportunity. I quickly slide the carabiner through Scotty's belt and shout, "GO!" Within seconds, Scotty is hauled up into the ceiling where he dangles, arms and legs flapping like a baby bird.

"Guys, come help me tie him off!" Dane calls from the wings. Toby and I run backstage to the pulley system and help Dane tie off the rope to the wall hooks.

"You let me down right this second, you little brats, or I'll . . ."

"Or you'll what?" I shout. "You don't seem to be in a position to make demands right now."

Scotty looks hilarious spinning around like some bizarre toy on a baby's mobile. It's like being threatened by a newborn. We all laugh at Scotty, which only makes him angrier. He thrashes and kicks and says some words that I'm not going to repeat.

TIP 28

SWEARING JUST MAKES YOU LOOK STUPID.

Swear words are for people who can't think of more intelligent words to use. When you're a stupid person in a stupid situation and you swear (especially at kids) you just look stupider!

"That's right," says Toby. "I'm not sure you could be in a worse position if you tried, actually."

This makes us laugh even harder, of course. Which makes Scotty thrash even more. Not a good move on his part, because suddenly his belt gives way a bit and his body falls forward. The rope pulls against his weight, sliding his trousers to his ankles and exposing some very unclean boxers with little hearts on them.

This is too much for us. We all lose it, laughing hysterically as Scotty dangles from his ankles above us in his stinky underwear.

His face is red as. I'm not sure if it's from anger, or the fact that he's hanging upside-down. Maybe a little of both.

"You can laugh now, you little brats, but I'll get down and when I do, I'm coming for you and your families!"

"I wouldn't be so sure about that," Sash's voice comes over the PA system. She switches on the light in the tech booth. There she stands, holding a microphone and staring down at Scotty.

"I did a bit of research. Yeah, Tess, you're not the only one who can Google." Sash winks at me. "Turns out, when you're on parole, if anything else pops up it can cause you a bit of trouble. So I'm sure you wouldn't want the police getting their hands on this . . ."

Sash pushes some buttons on the desk in front of her and a projector above the stage whirs to life. Scotty spins himself around and a video montage flickers on the screen. The soundtrack is some dumb song from that boy with the weird haircut she likes so much. Personally, I would have used "Bad Boys" by Inner Circle, but I can't really complain – the video is great. There's footage of Scotty taking money, beating up people and making shady deals, all shot from my bedroom window.

"Hey!" I say. "What happened to knocking?"

"Only applies to older siblings' rooms," Sash says. "And see that guy?" She pauses on a shot of Scotty shaking hands with some old guy and handing him a big wad of cash. "I Googled that guy. He's bad news, and there's a request out for information on anyone connected to him. So here's what I think. Are you listening, dirtbag?"

Scotty has stopped thrashing. The angry red has drained from his face. Now it's just upside-down red. He stares dejectedly at the screen.

"I think that you're going to stay far, far away from our family, from our friends and from our neighbourhood, and you're going to forget any of this ever happened. Because if you don't, I have a private YouTube link of this very video, complete with soundtrack, that I can email directly to the police. Do I make myself clear?"

Scotty nods.

"I wanna hear you say it," Sash says into the microphone.

"I'll stay away," Scotty says. "From all of you."

"Awesome!" Sash switches the tech room light off and heads downstairs. I high-five her as she joins us.

"Nice work, sis!"

Sash shrugs. "What-evs." And she pops her earphones in.

"Shall we get out of here?" says Toby, picking up the bag of fake money.

"Um, I'd leave that here if I was you," Dane suggests.

"What? Why?"

WOOF, WOOF! Butthead charges into the theatre with something black clenched between his teeth. He runs up to Dane, who bends down to hug him.

"Aw, who's a good boy?" Dane coos. "Did you bring me what I asked for, did you? Yes, you did! You're a good boy." Butthead drops the black thing at Dane's feet. It's some sort of rubber object, dripping with dog drool.

"What's that?" I ask.

"Scotty might recognise it," Dane says, looking up at the trouser-less bad guy spinning above us. Scotty frowns and then realises.

"Is that my—"

Police sirens wail in the distance.

"My ankle monitor!"

Dane grins. "Looks like he found a way to slip out of it and leave it at his mum's, so he can get around. His mum's house is on my delivery route, so I knew where he was at. All it took was a little doggy smarts and a game of fetch. Lucky an ankle monitor looks just like a big FitBit."

Dane turns to me. "I told you he was as smart as Mr Piddles. Now, say thank you to Butthead, Scotty. He brought your toy back to you."

WOOF!

The police sirens are getting louder.

I shake my head in disbelief. "I never thought I'd say this, Dane, but you're a genius." I bend down to pat Butthead. "And you . . . you're really not such a Butthead after all."

"Shhhh," says Dane. "It's a family secret. Now let's get out of here before the cops arrive."

"Definitely!" I look up at Scotty. "Now remember, one word about any of this to the cops and they get our little video." Scotty nods but he looks miserable.

I drop Scotty's ankle monitor into the bag of fake money. Grabbing all our stuff, we sneak over to the fire exit just as the police burst through the main doors. We stop at the door for just a second to watch their faces as they find their bad guy neatly strung up and waiting for them.

Before I close the door behind me, I hear one of the cops say, "What's this, Scotty?"

He's holding up a handful of our printed cash. "Counterfeit money? Ooohhh, bad move – that's a federal offence. You're playing with the big boys now. You're going away for a long, long time."

I close the door with a smile. "A long, long time . . ." I like the sound of that.

23

Nasi Goreng

"I thought you guys had pizza?" Dad says as he spoons out four extra plates of nasi goreng for us.

"Ah, yeah, we did," says Dane. "But you know us. Always hungry."

"So true." Dad passes the plates to Mum and she passes them around the table like an edible conga line.

I'm actually starving. I feel like my stomach has finally settled, like that nervous twist in my gut has gone away and left a huge gaping hole that I'm keen to fill with Dad's delicious fried rice. A plate comes my way and I pass it to Kathy.

"Bon appetit," I say, "and thanks!"

"Any time, kiddo," she says. Kathy turns to my parents. "Thanks so much for having me for dinner, Mrs and Mr Heckleston."

"Jenny and Alik," says Dad. "And it's the least we can do for delivering our daughter back safely. It's hard to keep track of them all sometimes, you know. Easy to miss it when they go on little rescue missions." Dad gives Olivia a small frown.

Mum laughs. "Well, lucky she did or I'd be having boots and belts for dinner, locked up in that props room. I still have no idea how I managed to trap myself in there."

"Best not to think about it too much, Mum," I say. "You work such long hours, It's easy for silly things to happen, I guess."

"Well, not any more," says Mum.

"What do you mean?" I ask.

Dad reaches over and takes Mum's hand. "Your mum and I have been talking about it. With everything that's been going on, we think it would be great to have her around a bit more."

Mum smiles. "I'm going to cut back a bit at the theatre, guys. We got that grant we applied for and so they're getting an assistant in. Which means

I'll have extra help at the theatre, so I'll be able to help Dad a bit more at home and maybe make it to a few more family dinners. I miss your dad's cooking. I miss you guys." She runs her hand through Liv's hair and winks at me.

"What about end of month?" I ask.

"Don't worry, Tess. We've crunched the numbers. It will be fine. We won't cut your pocket money."

"I don't need pocket money," says Olivia.

"And I have a job anyway," agrees Dane.

"I actually make more interest on my savings account than you give me," I say.

Sash scoffs. "Well, you're not touching *my* pocket money!"

Mum shakes her head at us. "You really don't have to worry, guys. It'll just be good to hang out together more often."

Sash, Dane, Olivia and I smile at each other. Jake just chews on his plate.

"Sounds great, Mum," says Sash.

"Yeah, Mum, sounds awesome," I say and give her hand a squeeze. I grab my cup of water and raise it to the middle of the table. "To the Heckleston Hothouse." We all raise our cups and I nod to Toby and Kathy. "Including our special guests." Just as we "cheers" our glasses, there's a knock at the door and Toby's mums poke their heads in.

"We could smell that from down the road," calls Fara. "Got enough for two more mouths?"

"Always!" Dad laughs. "Come on in. Toby, Kathy, scoot down. Dane, get the stools."

Toby's mums squeeze in and more nasi goreng is loaded onto plates.

I look around the table. Despite everything, it's a good day. I may not have a million dollars, but I have my people.

TIP 29

YOUR PEOPLE ARE EVERYTHING.
That's it. In the end, when you take away all the unimportant things – the money, the stuff, all the things we spend too much time worrying about – the only thing that matters is your people. The ONLY thing.

Later that night, after everyone goes home, I help Mum pack the dishwasher. It's Dane's turn, but I don't care. It's nice to be with Mum – just us. I give her a hug as she rinses off the plates.

"What was that for?" Mum says, playing with my hair.

"Do I have to have a reason?"

"No, of course not." Mum smiles. "But normally you do."

"It's just an I-love-you hug. And a thank-you hug," I say, and go back to stacking the dishes.

"Thank you for what?"

"Just everything. It was cool having everyone over tonight."

"I agree." Mum passes me a plate. "It was great to see Kathy again too. She's looking much better. Much happier. After everything that happened, I'm glad."

I stop and turn to Mum. "What happened?"

"Well, she's had a strange life. When we went to school together, her family was the richest family in Watterson."

"What!?" I almost drop the plate I'm holding. "Kathy? Are you sure?"

"Oh yes. Her parents owned Watto Mall and were worth squillions. She and her brothers and sisters had everything. We were all super jealous of them."

At this point I'm struggling to keep my jaw off the ground. Kathy has siblings?

"What happened?" I manage to ask.

"When her parents passed away, there was a fight over the will. I guess Kathy sued her siblings for their share and won. It sort of tore the family apart."

"Wait, so she inherited the entire family fortune? Why is she living in a park?" I ask.

"I don't really know," Mum says, passing me the cutlery. "Different stories have floated around about bad investments, or gambling and what-not. But in the end, she lost everything. And of course, her siblings weren't talking to her, so there was no one to help when things got bad. Just goes to show you, Tess, money isn't everything."

I have about a million questions zooming around in my head, but mostly I can just hear Kathy's voice.

"I've made more mistakes than anyone."

All right, I'm going to admit it. Once, and once only.

Kooky Kathy and I have a lot in common.

24

Monday Morning

Monday morning at school is wonderfully uneventful and boring. At break, Mr Deery asks me to apply for the Student Council.

"It's not a paid position," he explains. "But you can actually make a difference, you know. They have fundraisers, and help teachers make decisions about the school. They even put together that petition to keep Kathy's Lego house in Brennan Park. I know it's not really your thing but—"

"I'd love to, Mr Deery," I say, snatching the clipboard out of his hand and writing my name down. "Not everything is about money, right?"

He looks kind of stunned. I guess he thought I would take a bit more convincing. "No," he says. "It absolutely is not. That's great, Tess. Just great."

Toby has rehearsal at break. He's going to do the talent show this term. Yeah, seriously! Apparently Kathy has been teaching him some guitar and . . . wait for it . . . he's going to SING! I'm trying my best to be supportive and not make fun of him, but it's SO hard. I have this image of him getting up on stage and just freezing and doing his Chihuahua thing. But Kathy says he's actually really good. I've been wrong once or twice before, so I guess we'll see.

I grab my lunch and sit under a tree at the top playground. Lost in my thoughts, I almost don't notice Olivia slide in next to me. She's very quiet.

"Hey, Liv. Thanks again for your help yesterday. You were amazing. And I'm sorry I didn't include you from the beginning. I should have."

"Is it because of my diabetes?" she asks softly.

I don't want to lie to her, so I think about it hard. I shake my head.

"I don't think so," I say honestly. She looks at me doubtfully. "I mean it, Liv. I think it's because you're my little sister. Whether you have diabetes or not, I think I'm always going to want to protect you. It's sort of built in, you know?"

She smiles. "I guess I'd be the same with Jake."

"Exactly! But you're right, I can still involve you and protect you at the same time. Although maybe it's you who's going to be looking after me."

Olivia laughs. "Yeah, you don't think things through very much sometimes."

"Oh gee, thanks, Liv."

Her smile goes away and she frowns a little. "It's something we have in common."

"What do you mean?"

She takes my hand. "I have to show you something, Tess."

Olivia leads me to her classroom and checks there are no teachers about. She takes me to the back storeroom and opens the door. Piles of old toys and notebooks and stuff that looks like it hasn't been used for years fills the cupboard. Kneeling down, she grabs a plastic crate, sliding it out towards her. She pulls a couple of older, torn picture books from the top . . . to reveal two plastic shopping bags full of money.

"YOU took it?" I barely get the words out. I mean, I had no idea what happened to the money but . . . Olivia?!

She nods sheepishly. "I'm so sorry, Tess. I just wanted to be involved. To be a part of it. And you and Toby kept shutting me out. So I started listening in at your door and it didn't take long to work out what was going on."

"But, Liv, why would you just take it? It's so not like you."

"I thought maybe I could pay someone to fix me. I mean, I know there's no cure for diabetes, but, you know, I could buy a pump or give money to a doctor for the research. I thought if they could fix me, I wouldn't be different, and you guys wouldn't leave me out of things. I could go to birthday parties and eat cake and go straight to lunch at school without having to wait for my insulin."

I can see her eyes getting wet and there's a serious ache in my chest. So I'm either having a ten-year-old heart attack, or my heart is breaking for my little sister. I grab her and squeeze her.

"OK. Look, Liv. Firstly, being seven and having to deal with all this totally sucks, but you're the coolest, strongest kid ever, and you'll never let this diabetes thing hold you back. Secondly, I'm sorry. From now on you're in on everything, OK? A Heckleston Huddle is a Heckleston Huddle. All of us. And lastly, you don't need fixing, Liv. Nobody's perfect. I know I'm not. But we don't need fixing. Look at Dane. He's a doofus. And there's no cure for that, right?"

Olivia laughs softly and wipes at her tears. "I know you don't actually believe that after yesterday."

"OK, fine. He's not THAT doofus-y. But it doesn't matter, because we've got this weird-as family who loves us no matter what. You're my little sister and I wouldn't change a single thing about you, OK?"

She smiles and gives me a hug. "OK."

"So how about we get this money out of here? And no more secrets, all right?"

"No more secrets," Olivia agrees.

We grab the bags and take them to my locker. The locker's too skinny to fit the bags while they're full, so we check no one's watching and tip the money bundles in, shutting the door quickly before it all spills out.

"What are you going to do?" Olivia asks.

I shrug. "Same thing I always do. Ask Toby."

"Give it back!" Toby says.

"But what if we—"

"Give it back."

"OK, but maybe some of it could—"

"GIVE. IT. BACK." Toby isn't having any of it. And he's right. I know that. I do. But sometimes I just need someone to help point my moral compass in the right direction. He's sort of like my Jiminy Cricket. You probably don't know who that is. Googling won't help much because it will just tell you he's a talking cartoon cricket, but he's kind of a conscience for a character called Pinocchio and he tells him the right thing to do.

Pinocchio's an old 2D Disney movie, so you probably haven't seen it. It's kind of weird actually. But I'm sure Pixar will do a remake soon so maybe just hold off until then.

Toby's still glaring at me with his arms folded. "For once in your life, will you please just listen to your best friend? Didn't you learn anything from the last few weeks?"

"Yeah," I say. "I learnt that my best friend can be a real bossy boots when he wants to."

Toby smiles and unfolds his arms. "So?"

"Fine!" I say, throwing in an eye roll for good measure. "I'll give it back."

Toby puts his arm around my shoulders. "Great decision, Tess!" he says as we walk down the corridor.

"So you're coming to the head's office with me, then?" I ask.

He drops his arm and runs off in the other direction, his backpack bouncing behind him. "Nope, that's all you!" he calls over his shoulder. "I'll stay here and keep an eye on the money till you get back."

Thanks, Toby! Great best friend he is.

25

The Beginning of the End

So I'm walking down the school corridor – I'm pretty sure in slow motion – a look of determination on my face. I always look determined. Other kids stand in front of their lockers gawking at me as I pass. I ignore them, staring straight ahead. There's probably some theme music playing. Something like "Money" by Pink Floyd. On one side of me is my teacher, Mr Deery, and on the other the headteacher, Mrs Keiren. They're flanked by two police officers. Sound familiar?

Yep, that's right. This is where I get busted. I told you it would happen.

They open my locker and the million tumbles out. OK, so it's not a million any more. I'm sorry I lied at the beginning but "a million dollars" just rolls off the tongue easier than the eight hundred and whatever thousand it is now after our spending spree. So, money falls out, everyone gasps, I'm busted. I told you there were no surprises. I'm going to summarise the next bit because it's all pretty predictable.

My parents get called to the school.

There's a big discussion in the head's office with the police.

I tell them bits of what happened: I found the money, I spent a bit, I gave it back.

I skip over the kidnapping of my mother, the run-in with the bad guy and the involvement of ANY of my family members. Or Kathy. Fortunately, I was right about no one reading the local newspaper as no one mentions the donation photo. Those papers are probably just lining a whole bunch of cat-litter trays.

Toby, however, turns himself in. Seems he's a good best friend after all.

Toby explains that he kept a complete track of all our spending and hands over his accounts book and every receipt.

The police decide that because no one was hurt, and the money wasn't stolen but found, and that we had mainly done charitable things with it AND turned ourselves in, we were free to go.

This was all after a long lecture from the police. And then Mrs Keiren. And then our parents.

Then we got to go home.

$

I'm lying in bed writing my list.

There's been a lot of discussion about what my punishment should be. Mum and Dad must have been reading some new-age parenting book, because here's what they want me to do: write a list of all the things I did wrong – all the rules I broke, the bad decisions I made – then decide my own punishment for each thing. They said they don't want to see the list, they just want to know my final decision about the punishments.

Yeah . . . seriously.

And the list so far isn't making me feel very good about myself.

BAD THINGS LIST:
1) Talking to Scotty
2) Not telling anyone about the money
3) Taking the money
4) Spending the money
5) Getting Toby involved
6) Putting Olivia in hospital
7) Being mean to Olivia
8) ~~Stealing~~ ~~Borrowing~~ Taking Mum's driving licence and birth certificate without asking
9) Getting Kathy to lie for me
10) Opening a bank account in Mum's name
11) Making counterfeit money (Technically this was Toby, but who are we kidding? He never would have done this if it wasn't for me.)
12) Putting Toby, Kathy, Mum, Dane, Sash and Olivia ALL in danger

I'm feeling pretty overwhelmed when Mum comes in.

"How's it going?" she asks.

"Not great," I say. "I think grounded for life is probably fair punishment. Or jail."

Mum gives me a sad smile. "Well, before you settle on that, I want you to make me another list too. Make one of all the good things you did."

I look at my desk. "It might be a short list."

"Maybe," Mum says. "But make it anyway." And she leaves my room.

I rule a line down the middle of my page and start on the other side.

GOOD THINGS LIST:

1) Getting a bouncy castle for the kids at school
2) The coffee and doughnuts for the teachers (turns out Mr Deery LOVES the jam-filled ones)
3) The kids' hospital donations (that really was a great day)
4) Kathy's Lego house
5) The Guide Dogs donation (helping puppies is ALWAYS good)

6) The goat in Afghanistan
7) The orangutan we adopted in Borneo
8) The books and money and loads of other stuff we donated
9) Working together with Sash and Dane and Olivia
10) Saving Mum
11) Putting Scotty back in jail
12) Getting to know Kathy (OK, OK, she's pretty cool)
13) Making up with Olivia
14) Getting Sash to anonymously send the Scotty video to the police to double his sentence
15) FINALLY taking Toby's advice and giving the money back

Mum sticks her head back in my room. "Well?"

I look at my lists. They're actually pretty even. "OK, maybe not jail, but grounded for life still works," I say.

Mum stays at my door. "Here's the important question, though, Tess. How many things on the bad list would you do again?"

I don't even have to think about it. "None."

"And what about the stuff on the good list?" she asks.

I look at my list. "All of them."

Mum nods. "ok, well, your dad and I will have a think about the grounded for life thing and get back to you."

I crawl into bed and Mum tucks me in. "Good night, Tess. I love you." She kisses me on the forehead. "Can I pick you a song?" I nod. She flicks through my MP3 player and chooses something. "Your Song" by Elton John plays softly as she leaves my room.

It's nice being tucked in again.

26

A New Leaf

TIP 30

WE ALL MAKE MISTAKES. LEARN FROM THEM AND CHANGE.

I made a lot of mistakes. Made a lot of bad decisions. But I vowed to change. I decided that being honest and telling the truth was the best way to go. From that day forward I vowed to tell the truth, the whole truth and nothing but the truth.

BRING, BRING!

The landline? Seriously? This is the twenty-first century, guys. Call a mobile!

We're just about to sit down for dinner. Mum grabs the phone.

"Oh, hi, Senior Detective McKenzie." She shoots me a disapproving look. She hasn't quite forgiven me yet. "Yes, she's right here. I'll pop it on speaker phone."

"Hi, Tess, can you hear me?"

"Yep." Another dirty look from Mum. "Yes, Detective McKenzie."

"ok, so we've almost finished tying everything up, and I just want to confirm a few things with you."

"ok."

"So we've taken the money that was handed in and crosschecked it with the money spent according to the ledger and receipts that Toby gave us. He kept an excellent record of everything, which made it easy."

"Yep, that's Toby."

"So there was eight hundred thousand dollars recovered from your locker, and the receipts show that you guys spent and donated one hundred thousand. So that means that the original amount you found was nine hundred thousand dollars."

I pause.

"We've spoken to Toby, and he confirms that this is correct. We just need confirmation from you and we can wrap this whole thing up."

I don't say anything.

"Tess? Can you confirm for me that the original amount was nine hundred thousand dollars?"

I swallow. Why would Toby say that? He must have had a good reason.

My mum nudges me. "Answer him!" she growls.

I think about Toby "keeping an eye on the money for me" while I ran to get the head. He'd had his backpack with him. Had he . . . ? I chew on my lip. I have to say something. I decide that my solemn oath to tell the truth, the whole truth and nothing but the truth . . . will start tomorrow.

"Yes, Detective McKenzie, that's right. We found nine hundred thousand dollars."

There's a knock at the front door. Dad opens it and there stands Toby, looking pretty sheepish.

"Well, if it isn't Tess's partner in crime," Dad says, frowning at Toby. Clearly he hasn't quite forgiven us either.

"We came over to apologise, didn't we, Toby," Fara says, appearing behind him and shoving him through the door.

"I'm really sorry, Mr Heckleston," Toby says.

"Well, somehow I suspect you weren't the mastermind behind this one." Dad glares at me over his shoulder. "And it's Alik, Toby. Please." Dad and Fara head into the kitchen to no doubt commiserate over their delinquent children.

Toby and I hover in front of the TV. I really want to ask him about the money, about why he lied, but we aren't out of earshot of our parents.

"Can we go upstairs?" I ask.

"No way," Mum says. "Dinner's almost ready, and we're keeping our eyes on you two for the next decade. No more schemes."

Toby and I roll our eyes at each other and flop onto the sofa. With little else to do, we stare at the news on the TV. A reporter whose hair has so much hairspray in it that he looks like a Lego man pops up on the screen.

"In other news today, a feel-good story. Online charity watsi.org has been astonished by a one hundred thousand dollar donation from an anonymous source. Over three hundred patients in developing countries will receive much needed life-saving surgery, thanks to this generous donation."

I look at Toby. For once it's me doing the gold-fish thing. His mouth curls up at the corners as the reporter continues.

"It is estimated that over four hundred million people around the world lack access to essential health care. This money will change a lot of lives. It takes someone very special to care about people this much."

Toby moves his hand to his shirt and runs his finger over the scar on his chest. I reach down, take his other hand, and give it a squeeze.

"It sure does," I whisper.

I have the *best* best friend ever. And I'm glad my truth telling oath doesn't start until tomorrow.

TIP 31

YOUR DECISIONS ARE YOURS. MAKE THEM AND THEN OWN THEM.

People try to tell you that right and wrong is easy. It's not. It's not black and white – there's a whole lot of grey in the world. I'm not perfect, far from it. So maybe you shouldn't be listening to my tips anyway. Maybe you should be making your own. So here's my last one, take it or leave it.

You will make a lot of decisions in your life. Some good. Some bad. But they're yours. The person you are is made up of those decisions: by how you treat people, by the things you do. In the end, there's only one thing you can hope for.

At the end of the day, when you're lying in bed with the lights off with nobody to answer to except that little voice inside, you need to be proud of the person you are and fall asleep knowing you did the best you could.

"Are you holding my hand?" Toby says, totally breaking the moment.

"No," I say. I let go and shove him in the shoulder. Toby bursts out laughing and I can't help but join in.

"What are you two up to?" Mum shouts from the kitchen.

"Nothing!" I call back. I have so many questions for Toby. So many. But I know they'll have to wait.

I pick up the TV remote. "All right, enough listening about do-gooders." I switch over to the music channel. Flashback Fridays is on. My favourite.

"Dumb Things" by Paul Kelly is playing.

Toby grins at me. "How appropriate," he says.

"You can talk!" I reply.

Truth is, it's a great song. And it really is a perfect way to end this story. So Google it. Listen to it play as you imagine Toby and me sitting on the sofa, our parents chatting away in the kitchen. Turn it up a little louder. Toby bops from side to side, I roll my eyes at him, and we fade to black.

The End
(for real this time)

Secrets of a Schoolyard Millionaire

TIP 15   108
DON'T BE AN IDIOT. NO ONE LIKES AN IDIOT.

TIP 16   113
THE BLUES BROTHERS MOVIE IS COOL.

TIP 17   120
DON'T PUNCH PEOPLE.

TIP 18   121
IT'S NOT THAT EASY TO SPEND A MILLION DOLLARS
WHEN YOU'RE TEN. (EVEN WHEN YOU WANT TO DO
GOOD WITH IT.)

TIP 19   129
YOU SHOULD FOLLOW RULES BECAUSE YOU BELIEVE
THEY ARE RIGHT. NOT JUST BECAUSE THEY ARE SO.

TIP 20   134
"A MANAGER IS NOT A PERSON WHO CAN DO THE WORK
BETTER THAN HIS MEN. HE IS A PERSON WHO CAN GET
HIS MEN TO DO THE WORK BETTER THAN HIM."

TIP 21   149
WORRY LESS ABOUT WHETHER SOMETHING IS A LIE AND
MORE ABOUT WHAT THAT LIE WILL DO.

TIP 22   158
NO ONE CAN RESIST PUPPIES.

Did You Know...

... that Watsi is a real charity? Like Tess explains in the book, Watsi raises money to provide healthcare for people in need through crowdfunding. As of 2021, they've successfully funded life-changing operations for over 22,000 people and counting.

In fact, all of the donations that Tess and Toby make – including the Guide Dogs donation, gifting a goat, adopting an orangutan and sending books to underprivileged children – are inspired by charities that exist in the real world.

Check them out!

About Nat Amoore

Nat Amoore is a rather interesting person. Her secret superpower (shhh!) is making stuff up. Can you guess which Nat-Facts are true?

1) Nat ran a lot of her own money-making schemes when she was a kid.
2) Nat has a brother called Dane, who had a dog called Butthead.
3) Nat grew up on a small farm with sheep, chickens, cows, horses, rabbits, cats, dogs,

ferrets, a donkey, a goat and a pet kangaroo called Skippy.

4) Nat used to be a trapeze artist.

5) Nat is a host of *One More Page*, a podcast all about kids' books.

6) Nat (despite being kind of grown up) still sucks her thumb.

7) Nat's skills include juggling, tying balloon animals, waterskiing, making people laugh so hard their drink comes out their nose, and fire breathing.

8) Nat was on a reality TV show and she won.

9) Remember the prank with the clocks that Casey Wu wanted to do? Nat actually did that when she was at school.

10) Nat has been to over 40 countries – and eaten a whole lot of unusual food along the way.

11) Nat once got attacked by a moose and is now terrified of them!

12) Nat found a million dollars when she was ten but, unlike Tess, she gave it back.

Turn the page to find out which facts Nat made up!

About Nat Amoore
...the Answers

How many did you get right?

1) TRUE! Some of the schemes in the book are based on things Nat did as a kid. She refuses to admit which ones . . .

2) FALSE! Nat *does* have a brother called Dane, but his dog's name was Red Dog. She thinks that's just as ridiculous a name, though.

3) TRUE! The farm was a pretty cool place to grow up.

4) TRUE! Nat ran away and joined the circus when she finished school and spent many years travelling the world as a trapeze artist.

She only fell a few times, but she almost always landed in the net.

5) TRUE! Along with her writing buddies Kate and Liz, Nat loves to chat about all things kids' books. Check it out at onemorepagepodcast.com.

6) TRUE! Sucking her thumb is a habit Nat's never been able to kick. Some people laugh at her, but what if it's the key to her superpower and she wouldn't be able to write such awesome stories if she stopped? She is *not* willing to take that chance.

7) FALSE! Nat hasn't quite mastered fire breathing yet. She keeps setting her nostril hairs alight.

8) FALSE! She *was* on a reality TV show but she didn't win. And she doesn't want to talk about it.

9) TRUE! But don't tell her mum!

10) TRUE! Nat's eaten snake, chicken's feet, snails, an octopus that was still moving, crickets, worms, frogs' legs and SPAM!

11) FALSE! She did get attacked by a moose, but she made friends with it after. What she *is* scared of is jellyfish – they totally freak her out!

12) FALSE! As if she would give a million dollars back. Would you?

Want to know more about Nat? Follow **Tip 1** and GOOGLE HER!

Or, because being efficient is also important in business, you could just visit Nat's website: **natamoore.com**